# One Man to Beat

## Dr. Arnold Burron

Diamond Peak Press
Greeley, Colorado

# One Man to Beat

Queries may be directed to the author at
6437 24th Street, Greeley, Colorado 80634,
via phone/fax at 970 330 8206, or via e-mail
at Mountainavenue@aol.com

Cover illustration by Jillian Kay Melchior

Manufactured in the United States of America

ISBN 0-9673697-2-X

# One Man to Beat

## Contents

**Chapter**

# Chapter One: The Underdog Bites

There was one man to beat. This had been a wild contest with first one team, then the other, getting the surprise of their lives. And now, with 7 seconds on the clock, and the score tied 1-1, I could see only one guy between me and paydirt. I could hear the crowd screaming, "Go! Go! Go!" as I reached back, swept up the clearing pass, and spurted across the red line into the Warriors' territory. Biggy Benzin, the Warriors' star defenseman, was waiting for me. He had cut across from the left point, raced to his own end, pivoted into position, and, without losing a stride, was facing me, positioned for his favorite move, a poke check.

I hit the blue line at full speed. I was dangling the puck tantalizingly further in front of me than was safe, but I knew what he would do. Sure enough, Biggy's stick shot out like a striking rattler, but I was ready. I literally sucked in my gut, pulled the puck back, and swept around him. Their goalie didn't have a chance. Nobody had ever beat the Warriors' big defenseman one-on-one, so the goalie was braced for a shot from the blueline. When I danced around Biggy and swooped in on goal, I caught the goalie out of the net, trying to cut down the angle for a long shot. Before he knew what happened, he was flat on his hind end at the top of the crease, the puck was tucked into back corner of the net, and our fans were going absolutely bananas.

With only one second on the clock, the refs didn't bother with a faceoff. Our box had erupted with unrestrained celebration, as guys tumbled over the boards and pummeled me in frenzied ecstasy. We had beaten the Warriors! And we were in the playoffs! The team that everybody said had no chance against the top team in the league had beaten them! We would be playing for the provincial championship! We had squeaked in!

This game was a *must win* for us, because we didn't have that great of a record during the regular season. Maybe the Warriors were overconfident. Maybe we were just on fire! Maybe they had a bad game! Maybe it was pure luck, or a fluke. Whatever it was, it didn't matter. All that counted was that we had won, 2-1! David had beaten Goliath.

It had been an absolutely crazy game. The Warriors probably should have destroyed us in the first period, but they couldn't get the puck past Demski, our goalie. Demski was an absolute fanatic. For one thing, he had this terrible temper, and if you got him mad, watch out! He would turn into a crazy man. Well, some of the Warriors had been trying to rattle him before the game, on the way into the arena, calling him "Dumb-ski." If there was one thing he couldn't take, it was that. Maybe it was because he wasn't too great in school. Anyway, when he heard "Dumb-ski," he had about gone ballistic. If our coach hadn't been there to restrain him, he probably would have gotten into a fistfight. As it was, he was red in the face and fuming all through warmups, and I think his heat must have caught us all on fire. Coach Arnold had grabbed Demski and yelled, "Look, if you want to shut 'em up, the best way to do it is to be a brick wall in goal. Don't shut them up! Shut them *out*! *Get* mad! *Be* mad!

*Stay* mad! Get them so frustrated that they won't know whether they're coming or going! Teach 'em a lesson, 'Dem'. Shut their mouths by shutting 'em out!"

And shut 'em out he did! By the time Demski hit the ice, he was like a maniac. In warmups, he was blocking shots, kicking away rebounds, and yelling like a madman. I thought he was out of his mind. And he played the same way. The Warriors came out like the undefeated team they were. They acted like they owned the ice; like, if they put their sticks on the ice, we were supposed to fall down and give up. But they shouldn't have riled Demski.

From the opening faceoff, they had us scrambling to get the puck out of our zone. Their defensemen were a wall on our blueline, and we couldn't get anything started. We would no sooner get the puck out, and there would be a turnover and we'd be back in our own end. It seemed to be raining pucks, but Demski the madman turned away shot after shot, screaming at them, screaming at us, and screaming at nothing in particular. All of a sudden the crowd got into it, and even people who hadn't picked sides started cheering every time Demski made a save.

Maybe it was total frustration. Whatever it was, the Warriors started to take bad shots. They pressed too hard. Their defensemen pinched in too far off the blueline, and, before anybody knew what happened, a bouncing puck turned into a clearing pass, a breakaway for us, and the first goal!

That, really, was the turning point. The Warriors lost their discipline. You could almost see their frustration when, rush after rush, shot after shot, Demski kept turning them away. Something had definitely happened to them.

And something happened to the rest of us. Sometime during the First and Second Periods, we became believers. We could see a look in the Warriors' eyes that was a look of panic. They couldn't score! They just, plain, couldn't score! We were ahead, 1-0, and there were six minutes left in the game. If we could just hang on!

And then it happened. Demski took a puck right in the neck, went down, and wasn't able to cover up. In the scramble, the puck slithered across our goal line, and the score was tied! They had broken through the dam!

What I remember of the rest of the game is weird. It was like there was no sound--

nobody in the arena, no noise when the puck hit the boards, no nothing. Like turning off the volume on TV. How we made it to those last few seconds I couldn't tell you. All I remember is that when the sound came back on it was a huge roar. I had the puck, and it seemed like the whole arena was exploding with cries of "Go! Go! Go!"

I think that maybe I was the only one in the whole place who wasn't surprised when I beat Biggy and slammed the puck home. The end of that game was the perfect moment for me. Except for one thing. I don't know what made me look toward the Warriors' bench, but I did. And at precisely that moment, I caught Biggy Benzin glaring at me. He was mouthing something. I couldn't hear a thing over the commotion around our bench, but there was no mistaking what he was saying: "You're dead meat!" he mouthed, menacingly pointing his gloved hand at me.

To be honest, that took a bit of the edge off. Because if there was anything you could say about Biggy Benzin--"Bully, cocky, big mouth, dirty player, unanimous all star"--all of which he was, there was one thing you couldn't call him. A quitter. He had a reputation of making life miserable for any opponent who crossed him. But I had no idea, at that moment, how miserable life was going to be.

I had other things to think about.

## Chapter Two: An Unexpected Problem

Usually, I think I can handle just about anything, if I know what I'm up against. I don't mean that I don't sometimes get scared, or nervous, or stuff like that. But if I know what to expect, I can handle it. Like when we first came to Manitoba, Canada, from Wyoming.

My Dad was in the military. That means transfers. So, one thing I was always sure about, from first grade on, was that, sooner or later, I'd be the new kid in school. When I was a little kid, it wasn't a big deal--you know, "Here's your tote box, sit at this table." I could almost predict what the new teachers would say. "Class, this is Nathan. Nathan is from blah-blah-blah. Nathan, can you tell us about blah-blah-blah?" That was supposed to make me feel welcome, but I always hated it, because everybody would be looking at me.

Even though I hated it when everybody's looking at me--still do, in fact--I could mumble a few words about my school and my teacher, and that was it. Upper grades were harder, but still no big deal. Everybody stares at you when you walk in. Some kids will be real friendly right off, but that's usually because they have no friends, so they'll latch on to anybody. A few kids will act stupid to show off. And then, of course, certain girls will whisper to each other and giggle in a way that you can't tell whether they're saying, "Neat," or "Nerd."

All that stuff I can take. Because I know what to expect. I even know that some kid will always act like a bully, and, sooner or later, he'll be in my face. I don't like it, but, like I said, I can handle just about anything if I know what to expect.

So I wasn't too worried showing up for school in Manitoba, even though, when I left Wyoming, my teacher and classmates at Faith Christian School had a special day for me. Mr. Tunn, who was usually a really cool guy, had made the class stand in a circle on my last day at Faith, and have a special prayer for me. I don't remember what most of the kids said, because it was kind of embarrassing being the center of attention, but I can still remember what Mr. Tunn said.

"Lord," he began, "be with Nate as his family joins his Dad in Manitoba. Be with him as he faces unexpected problems in a new country and a new school. Help him to be a faithful witness to those who don't know you."

Mr. Tunn said some other stuff, too, but I have to admit that I haven't got a clue what it was, because I got stuck on that one expression in his prayer. "Unexpected problems in public school." And in that one sentence, one word stood out: "Unexpected."

Like I said, usually I can handle anything if I know what to expect. And I figured I could handle things like new kids, a lot bigger school, and way more students. I also figured that because there were so many kids, maybe it might be tough to make some of the school sports teams. None of that really bothered me too much. But there was one problem in that school that I didn't expect.

Schools in Manitoba had teams, just like in the states: soccer, football, basketball, and other sports. But when it came to hockey, that was a different story. High schools had hockey teams, but middle schools and junior high schools didn't have any. Hockey teams for kids my age had nothing to do with your school. If you were a hockey player, you could try out for any team you wanted to. So there could be two kids sitting in the same classroom who played for two totally different hockey teams. Usually, they'd try out for the same team, but a lot of times they'd end up on different teams in the same league.

A hockey league that had nothing to do with your school was something I didn't expect. Playing against kids who were in the same classes at school was a totally new idea. Although that was something I didn't expect, I didn't think it was going to be a problem.

I was soon to find out that I was wrong.

## Chapter Three: A Warning

Coach Arnold had warned me, after all of the excitement of getting into the playoffs had died down, that it would be especially important for me to keep my head up when we played the Warriors again.

"Nate," he had said, with a serious look on his face, "that was a fantastic move that you put on Biggy Benzin."

That was when I first found how proud Coach Arnold was. He wasn't at all like Mr. Tunn, at Faith Christian. Mr. Tunn would tell you, bigtime, if you did something good. Coach Arnold was exactly the opposite. His idea of praise was to just kinda' look at a guy, and sort of tip his chin downward. That meant that he liked what you did. Almost like somebody nodding a "yes." If a guy did something really fantastic, coach would add something to his look-and-nod.

He'd give a quick wink. But that was it. He just didn't praise people with words. Hollering, though, he could do, especially when somebody screwed up. Praise was another thing! So now that he was actually talking about something he liked, I was all ears.

"It was a good move, Nate, but I want you to be thinking about something," he said, seriously.

"Biggy's one of the toughest players in the league," Coach Arnold continued, "and he's a fast learner. One thing you can be sure of, Nate; he's going to remember who made him look like a clumsy beginner, and he's going to be looking for you. You injured his pride. He realizes that anybody who's really a hockey fan knows that you faked him out of his jockstrap!"

Coach Arnold brought to my attention what I should have known. Biggy would be waiting to get even. But I have to admit it, I hadn't thought about it. I had just kept re-playing that goal in my head.

I knew coach was right. Of course Biggy was embarrassed. He had been skating backwards, stooped low, with his stick in one hand, waiting to do what he always did best; namely, a poke check. He would let a rushing opponent move in on him, and, at the last second, his stick would flick out like a prairie rattler, and the onrushing forward would be puckless. Biggy would put on the brakes in a huge spray of ice chips, and in less time than it took for the stickhandler to realize that all he had on the blade of his stick was thin air, Biggy would be racing down the ice, swooping across the blueline, and roaring in on the defenseless goalie, letting loose with a vicious slapshot.

What Biggy didn't know was that I was prepared for him. I had watched the Warriors play, and I had especially watched him, because everybody was always talking about the Warriors' big captain. In fact, I had not only watched him. I had studied him.

So, when I made that rush, I deliberately carried the puck further ahead of me than usual. That was my "bait." The "switch" part of it was, at the instant that he shot out his poke check, I pulled the puck back toward me. Instead of his usual, "poke the puck loose, put on the brakes in a huge spray of ice chips, and break down the center," Biggy lurched forward like a guy falling off a ladder. The momentum that usually turned into a blazing rush down the ice threw him off balance as he tried to change directions at the last second. Instead of a glorious charge down the middle, Biggy Benzin awkwardly twisted around, seemed to trip over his own feet, and landed on his rear end, with his stick thrust high in the air like a circus clown's umbrella.

Coach Arnold's words made me feel like the time  when I was a little kid and I dropped an ice cream cone in a sandpile. That's how I felt.  Scoring the goal was the ice cream cone.   But Coach Arnold's warning was the ice cream flopping off the end of the cone into the sandpile. After coach's warning every time I tried to think about the goal, I ended up thinking about what kind of revenge Biggy would be looking for.

For sure, Biggy Benzin wasn't used to losing.  And he absolutely wasn't used to being faced. So I expected that he would try to get revenge on the ice.  But I didn't expect retaliation to take place at school.  What I saw at school, though, brought the words of Mr. Tunn's prayer back to mind.  Especially the "unexpected problems in public school" part.

They were definitely unexpected.  And they were definitely problems.

## Chapter Four: A Faceoff at School

I suppose it was about a week later when I got my first big shock at school. It was something I didn't expect to see. Well, to be more accurate, it was some*one* I totally didn't expect to see anywhere but on the ice, at the arena. Actually, I didn't so much see him, as sense him.

I was late for the first day of the second trimester, because of some stuff my family had to go through at Canadian immigration. I got to school just when first lunch hour was starting. I was always in class during first shift, so I really had never thought about who went to lunch at that time. As I'm making my way down the hall with all the noise and stuff, I suddenly notice that it's deadly quiet, even though the hall is packed with kids. And there was almost a path through the middle, like Moses going

16

through the Red Sea. Only, I didn't feel like Moses. I felt like one of Pharaoh's guys. I had a funny feeling in the pit of my stomach. And I knew, by the funny feeling in the pit of my stomach, that something was up, and that it had to do with me. Then I heard my name murmured from some kid in the crowd. At that moment, I figured that this whole deal meant trouble.

I could feel my face getting hot, and I knew it was turning red. That was the one thing I hated about myself more than anything--I couldn't hide my feelings over anything. If something was important to me, good or bad, sure enough, I'd turn red. Well, I knew I was as red as the backside of a baboon. It wasn't because I was afraid. It was because I wasn't expecting what I saw.

There, in the middle of the hall, hands on hips, feet apart, loomed Biggy Benzin. And he had a look on his face that said, "I know something you don't know." What he knew was something I didn't know until precisely that moment. We were in the same school! He also knew something else that I didn't find out until later that day. We were not only in the same school; we were in Miss MacIntyre's math class together.

Anyway, there stands Biggy Benzin, blocking my way. There wasn't any room to maneuver, but I tried, anyway. I acted like I was ignoring what was happening. I stepped to the side, to go around him. He moves to the side, almost like he's on defense, on the ice, and he blocks my way. I'm still trying to ignore him. I stepped back to my left, and Biggy steps to his right, blocking my way again. He was challenging me in front of everybody!

All this time, there's about twenty pairs of eyes staring at me, and absolutely no sound whatsoever in the hallway, except for some mocking snickering from a bunch of girls.

Biggy curled his lip up and kinda' hissed, "Fake your way out of this one, hot stuff." So, I'm standing there, trying to figure out what I'm going to do, short of whacking him, which wasn't a good idea because it was in school. In school, the penalty for fighting was automatic suspension, I didn't see a way out of this one. For sure, Biggy's buddies would swear that I started it. I couldn't just stand there. I was on the verge of being late for class. That might not sound like a big deal, but it was. The way they took attendance there, if you missed the morning session, and you were late for the afternoon, it counted as a whole day of absence. The big deal was, attendance was part of your grade. They called it "class participation," or some stupid thing. I was thinking about all this at about a hundred miles an hour, when Biggy's voice jarred me out of my thoughts of escape. He was kind of whining, in a mocking, sissy-sounding voice.

"Excuse me, Mr. Benzin, may I please pass?" Biggy prompted, in a tone intended to sound like a pleading little sissy. Again, the bunch of girls snickered, and Biggy's buddies just stood there with amused smirks on their faces.

If I could have acted like the whole episode didn't phase me, I could have probably pretended I was really calm. If I could've done that, I would have. But, like I said, my red face always gave me away. So everybody knew I wasn't calm. They just didn't know exactly what I was thinking.

"Excuse me, Mr. Benzin, may I please pass?" Biggy mocked again, in a sniveling tone.

There was no way I was going to call Biggy "Mr. Benzin" and ask him for permission to pass. Besides, I was mad!

Biggy might be able to beat the snot out of me--they didn't call him "Biggy" because he was a midget--but I figured I could get in one good punch, right where it hurt. If I got a good punch in, I figured that that some teacher would break up the fight before Biggy pulverized me. But I also knew that I would be the one to get suspended, because I knew that if I smacked him, his buddies would say I started it, and I'd be the one taking the punishment.

All this stuff is racing through my mind, and I could feel my fist clenching and my muscles tensing. I would fake a punch to his face, and when he lifted his hands, I'd plow him one right in the guts! It would be worth it!

Right in the middle of all these rushing thoughts, something odd happens. It's like I hear Mr. Tunn's voice, but, of course, it was only a thought in my own head: *"He who can control his anger is stronger than one who can take a strong city."* It was one of the verses from Proverbs echoing through my brain in tMr.Tunn's class. I could have been sitting back at Faith Christian school, in religion class, it was so real!

I could feel my muscles go slack. "Why should I play into his hands?" I thought.

20

Maybe hitting him hard and fast would temporarily solve my problem, but it would create a lot of other problems. Besides, I didn't have to go past Biggy. If I went back the way I came, and sprinted to class, I could still make it without being late.

Without a word, I spun around, tucked my books into the crook of my arm like a football, and took off down the hall, back the way I had come in. It was the long way around to class, but I would just make it on time.

Resisting the urge to smash him just once wasn't easy. As I sprinted for the door, all I could hear were taunts of "Chicken, chicken!" and a bunch of mocking laughter. I hate to think of how red my face must have been.

But when I think of what happened later to Demski, when Biggy and company made him lose his cool, holding my temper turned out to be a wise decision.

## Chapter Five: More Surprises

One other surprise that day was when I discovered that Biggy and I were in a couple of classes together. In the first class, I knew it before I even walked into the room. I was still in the hallway, about to go into class. I could hear a commotion in the room. Through the open doorway, I could see a bunch of kids laughing and carrying on in the far corner of the room.

In the middle of them, like a king surrounded by his subjects, sits Biggy. He was busy doing an imitation of one of our other teachers, Miss Macintyre, who taught French and Math. Nobody really noticed me come in. I was glad they didn't notice me. For sure, Biggy would have created a disturbance. Not that I was scared of him, but, like I said, I hate to be the center of attention, because my face would get red.

So I picked a seat close to the front of the room and quickly sat down, about a second before the history teacher, Mr. Cameron, walked in.

Now in Mr. Cameron's class, there was no goofing around. He had a reputation. He didn't put up with any nonsense whatsoever. Still, everybody liked him, because he made stuff interesting. He was strictly business, but he was fun. He would even allow a few student wisecracks. But if you were going to try to be funny, you'd better really be funny; because stupid jokes or wise-guy comments he would not put up with. You'd get "The Look." And deadly silence. And you'd feel like a fool.

Class would start the minute Mr. Cameron walked in. As soon as he hit the doorway, the room immediately got quiet. Nobody wanted to have to deal with Mr. Cameron. He never told anybody anything twice. So it was better to be quiet right off the bat. It kind of made you feel a little nervous, being in Mr. Cameron's class. One thing he'd do is ask a question, pause, wave his finger around in a big circle, and then suddenly point at you and spit out your name. You were expected to answer. If you gave a stupid answer, or, worse yet, no answer at all, he would usually have some remark about you that made you feel like you would rather have gone to the dentist that day.

I don't want to get off the subject, but besides Biggy Benzin, there was one other thing about Mr. Cameron's class that bothered me. There was this girl. Marlene. I think she was the first person I noticed after I sat down, although I'm not sure. And it wasn't that she was cute--which she definitely was! I think that what got me was that everybody was yackin' away, with one eye on the doorway watching for Mr. Cameron, but this girl seemed to be in a world of her own. All the other girls were in little groups, giggling and gossiping and kinda' checking the guys out, but this girl was different. Some of the boys were obviously trying to get her attention. If she noticed anybody in the room, she sure didn't let on that she did. I could only see the side of her face, because she was seated a little to the front of me, and also to the left. She seemed to be totally into some book she had. She acted like she couldn't see or hear anything or anybody. But as soon as Mr. Cameron came in, gone was the book, out came a notebook, and her attention was on the front of the room.

It's a good thing Mr. Cameron gave us a handout that first period, because I can honestly say I don't remember one thing he said. I think I was caught off guard. I didn't expect this. Biggy Benzin at the same school! And in a couple of the same classes! I couldn't see Biggy, because he was kinda' to the left of me, too, and a few rows back. But you know how you just know it when somebody is looking at you? I could feel him and his buddies glaring at me. It wasn't just my imagination, either. There was this one kid, Ned, that some of the kids called "Nerd." He was such a brain that nobody knew what he was talking about half the time. He was nice enough, but he didn't seem to have any friends. Ned's locker was right next to mine, and from the first day I came to Isaac Newton Public School, Ned latched onto me. Anyway, at the lockers, between classes, he said, "Man, you should've seen how Biggy was glaring at you. He hates your guts. Everybody's heard how you faced him so bad last week. He'll pull something on you if you don't watch it."

I'd be lying if I said that Ned's comments didn't bother me. Besides that, something else was bothering me even more. But in a different way. In all the commotion, when everybody was leaving class, I was looking down, pretended to be busy, to avoid Biggy and his buddies. After the noise died down, I picked up my stuff to leave. I figured that everybody was gone. But I was wrong. One person was still in the room. She was standing by the doorway. It was Marlene. She was looking straight at me. She didn't say a word. She just looked at me. Hard. And her eyes told me that if I thought she was in a world of her own, I was wrong. She wasn't. I was in it.

Before I even had time to think, she had turned, and she was gone.

For some reason, at that moment, I had trouble breathing. I felt like I was at the end of one of Coach Arnold's conditioning drills, doing wind sprints. All of a sudden, I couldn't wait to get back to Mr. Cameron's history class. Crazy thing was, I never really liked history class before.

## Chapter Six: Unexpected Visitors

I didn't have too much time to think about those eyes. That was probably good, because I'd be doing something or other, and all of a sudden I would see them, in my mind. I had this sortof picture in my head, of Marlene standing in the doorway, except that in the picture, I didn't seem to see anything but those eyes. I also didn't have too much time to think about what Biggy might try to pull in Mr. Cameron's history class. Making the playoffs had changed everything. During the season, we had two practices a week, and one on Saturday. Things were definitely different now.

The big game was two weeks away. We were now practicing every night of the week, over an hour at a crack. If anybody thought they were playing hockey for fun, forget it! Starts and stops were the worst.

Line up at center ice. Blast off at the whistle. Screech to a halt at the whistle. Blast off again. Stop again. Go again. Stop again. Crash into the boards. Race back to center ice. Cut left. Stop at the whistle. Cut right. Go! Stop! Guys would fall, and get screamed at. Some guys would hang onto the end boards puking over the side. It took only one practice to decide to skip an after school snack.

"Guts, Guts!" Coach Arnold would yell. "No pain, no gain!" In practice and in pep talks, Coach Arnold was full of sayings, most of which had more than one meaning. You could never be sure of what he meant. But there was no mistaking what he was after. It was the same lecture, in one form or another, before practice, during practice, and after practice:

"Now listen you guys, this is it. You can beat anybody you decide to beat. You gotta' want it so bad you can taste it. If your legs burn, make 'em burn more. You're not skating unless they're on fire. If you're screaming for air, go until you feel like you swallowed a blowtorch. When you hit somebody, hit him so hard that you see him spray spit. Whoever wants it the most will have it. The toughest opponent in the world is never the guy across the ice from you. It's yourself. If you conquer yourself, you can conquer anybody!"

Like I said, it was the same talk, in one form or another, every game.

I knew one thing for sure. We didn't have the best players in the playoffs. We didn't even have the best team in the playoffs. But with Coach Arnold, we would probably have one of the most motivated teams in the playoffs. And we would absolutely have the best-conditioned team. We would be able to outlast anybody.

Of course, being the best-conditioned meant that we would also be dragging our rear ends by the time practice was over. By the time I got to bed, the second my head hit the pillow, I was gone. That's why thoughts about Biggy didn't get much room in my head. Now, those eyes--well, that was a bit different. I have to admit that, without warning, my mind would flash a snapshot of those eyes looking at me from the doorway of Mr. Cameron's class. But that wasn't because I planned to think about them. They just popped into my head uninvited.

It wasn't just practice and being exhausted that kept my mind off Biggy Benzin and what he might pull in class. And it wasn't that this was the playoffs. There were rumors going around. Everybody had been saying for weeks that a professional scout was coming to town to watch the playoffs. He had been selecting players for what was called "Development Camp." The best 20 players in Saskatchewan and Manitoba would get to spend a week with the top hockey people in the country. Getting picked for Development Camp was a sure sign that the pros thought you had talent. Maybe you'd even have the potential to play professionally. The scout had come to check out our league just in time for the playoffs. Everybody was saying that the scout already had a list of names of prospects. Supposedly, he would be basing his final choices on how the players on his prospect list played in the playoffs.

If all this was true, I wanted to go to that camp. For once, I understood what Coach Arnold meant when he said that you had to want something so bad you could taste it. I could taste it. . Trouble was, nobody knew who was on the prospect list. Most people were pretty sure that Biggy Benzin was on the list. But he was the only sure thing. As far as who else was on the list, if anybody-- including the coaches--knew, they weren't telling. At least, they weren't telling until now. That was about to change.

What Coach Arnold said to us at the end of practice made me forget about hating starts and stops. I'd do them until Kingdom Come if I had to!

"Boys, I probably shouldn't tell you this, but I think you should know. The rumors you've been hearing about scouts coming to town are true. One of them is a guy I played with in the International Hockey League. He'll be here for sure, and maybe one or two others, for the playoffs. They're picking two or three players from every league. I've been told that they have a couple of spots for players from our league, for Development Camp if they find what they're looking for."

I didn't want to be stupid, so I didn't ask what they were looking for. I was afraid that Coach Arnold might say, "If you have to ask what they're looking for, you don't have it!" Worse yet, the people who were watching practice might ridicule me. I could almost hear it: "What are *you* asking that for? You think a scout would be interested in *you*?!" So I kept my mouth shut. But I made up my mind. Whatever they were looking for, I'd have it. And I thought I knew what it was.

Suddenly, practice became something else for me besides a reason to skip snacks so I wouldn't puke over the boards. Everything became deadly serious. When we did "three-on-twos," I couldn't have been more intense if we'd have been in a game. Every rush I took with my wingmen was playoff caliber. I wasn't kidding myself that I was putting out one hundred per cent. I'd go until my lungs felt like somebody was stabbing me in the chest, and until my calves and thighs were screaming for mercy.

"How you practice is how you play." That was Coach Arnold's all time favorite saying. He was full of sayings. Another one of his favorites was the one that kept ringing in my ears when we pulled a surprise upset at the beginning of the season against the Sharks. They were one of the biggest teams in the league. Man for man, they were a lot bigger and a lot meaner than we were. But it didn't matter. Every time I fought for a loose puck, every time there was a scramble in the goal crease, every time I had to go into the corners, I could hear Coach Arnold's words ringing in my head: "It's not the size of the dog in the fight. It's the size of the fight in the dog!" At first, I didn't know what he was talking about, but after hearing it about ten zillion times, I finally got it. I wasn't that big. But I made up my mind that I would be faster, tougher, and meaner than anybody on the ice.

Crazy as it seems, in that game we swarmed all over the place like a pack of pit bulls. Pound for pound the Sharks should have creamed us, but we totally out-hustled them and won the game. Somebody even kidded us about needing rabies shots!

There was one other reason I was practicing like a mad dog. There were two strangers watching us practice.

You could tell who was watching practice, because of the rink we practiced in. It was an old rink called the Olympic. It had been the first indoor rink in the interlake area, even though they didn't have artificial ice. They just didn't bother heating it, that's all. It was a good place to practice, since you could never get snowed out. But it had been long ago abandoned as a place for games. It was so old that they built the stands to seat only a few hundred people, and then only on one side of the rink. There was only one door from the lobby, too. So it would be hard for anybody to come in at a practice and not be noticed.

Not that I was daydreaming or looking around or anything, but we were doing rushes on the end that the lobby door was on. While I was waiting my turn, I noticed these two men standing at the end of the stands, in the shadows, near the exit. And when the door to the lobby swung open, there was enough light at the end of the stands to see that they were taking notes.

My heart started thumping in high gear! One of the men had to be Coach Arnold's buddy from Development Camp! In fact, both of them were probably from Development Camp! They had sent two scouts!

The rest of practice was like a playoff game for me. Since the scouts were there, I'd show them everything I had! And I did. I was first in the corners on dump-in practice. I hustled in every other drill we had. But the best, I saved for last. We were doing one-on-ones, and when it was my turn, I did my favorite move, the "bait and switch." I came tearing in on Conklin, our toughest defenseman. When I was only feet from him, I pushed the puck tantalizingly ahead of me, inches from Conklin's reach. As many times as Conklin had seen me do it, he still went for the bait, lunging for the puck with a fierce pokecheck. At the last second, I sucked it back, pulling in my gut at the same time, and danced around him. I swooped in on Demski, but I didn't score. Demski had come out of the net to cut down the angle, and I was going too fast to try to deke him out, and I shot wide. But it didn't matter. My stickhandling was what mattered. If the scouts were there, I'd show them everything I had.

I didn't find out until later that showing the strangers everything I had might have been a mistake.

A big mistake!

## Chapter Seven: Biggy Plays Dirty at School

I spent so much time thinking about the championship game coming up that school never entered my mind. Except, of course, for the class I was in with Biggy. I figured that sooner or later, he would try to pull something to get me into trouble. Worse yet, he might try to make me look stupid. If that happened in front of Marlene, the girl with the eyes, I would probably rather drop dead.

Walking into Mr. Cameron's classroom gave me the same kind of feeling in my stomach that I had before a big game.

The butterflies in my stomach didn't last very long, though. About the time I got my stuff out of my backpack, Mr. Cameron comes bouncing through the doorway, and the lesson began. He was one of those teachers who started teaching the minute he entered the room. Everybody paid attention, too, not just because he didn't put up with any nonsense. It was because he usually started off with something interesting. There's no "Good morning," or anything. He just starts in like he's been there all day, and like he just paused to take a breath. Another thing is his desk is at the back of the room, instead of the front, so he can see exactly what's going on during the ten minutes or so that he gives us to get started on our homework.

Today was no different. Almost before I opened my notebook, he starts in.

"Most of you kids are up on sports," Mr. Cameron declared. "But I wonder if any of you can answer this question: 'Who knows the nickname of the Minnesota's football team in the NFL?'"

"Duh-uh," somebody mutters from the back of the room. "The Vikings."

"Okay," Mr. Cameron says, "I don't know who the wise guy is, but let's see if you can answer this one."

Mr. Cameron strolled to his desk at the back of the room, talking as he made his way down the aisle. "Who knows how the Vikings got their name?"

This time there wasn't any wise guy comment. Everybody sat there, waiting for what Mr. Cameron would come out with next.

"I didn't think so," he said, turning to the corner where the "Duh-uh," had come from. "Even Mr. Duh-uh doesn't know that one."

Everybody laughed. Mr. Cameron had a way of putting people in their place, even when they thought they had gotten away with something.

"Here's what happened," he smiled, after the laughter had died down. "In 1848, a farmer got his plow stuck on a huge stone in a field in northern Minnesota. The stone had markings on it that talked about some explorers. The explorers had sailed through what is now Manitoba and Minnesota."

"Vikings!" somebody blurted.

"Right!" Mr. Cameron continued, pulling down the wall map and really getting into it, sweeping his hand down from Manitoba to Minnesota. "In your text, you'll find a discussion of Kensington Runestone. It'll tell you about the Vikings.

"There are a lot of other team names that come from geography or history. There are names that come from places or events.

They describe something that happened, or what something looks like."

Mr. Cameron paused, looking around. "For example," he continued, "Biggy, c'mon up here."

By this time Mr. Cameron was at the front of the room, at the chalkboard.

"Now take Biggy," Mr. Cameron said, walking a few steps away from him, and gesturing. "He's a big kid for his age. Hence, 'Biggy.'"

Mr. Cameron tossed a piece of chalk to Biggy. "Let's see how many nicknames the class can think of. Biggy, you write 'em down. I'll start it off. 'Calgary Stampeders!'"

"Dallas Cowboys!" somebody piped up.

"49' ers! The Gold Rush of 1849 in San Francisco," Ned offered.

Everybody looked at Ned like he was some kind of weirdo, since he was the only kid in class who would have known that kind of thing. In fact, the reason he was called 'Nerd' was that he was such a brain, and most of the kids were just plain jealous of him.

"Ned's right," Mr. Cameron explained. "There was a gold rush in 1849 near San Francisco, California. Now, there are a lot of other names you can read about. Biggy, put these on the list."

Mr. Cameron rattled off a whole bunch of team names like he was a sports encyclopedia. "'Padres.' 'Seventy-Sixers.' 'Canucks.' 'Argonauts.' Here's one that will surprise you: "'Los Angeles Lakers,' They were called the 'Lakers' because they started off in the state that has a lot of lakes, and then they moved to California."

By this time, Mr. Cameron had us. We were all ready to read the assignment, but he continued.

"Okay, can anybody think of any other nicknames?"

After about five seconds of no responses, Biggy turns to Mr. Cameron, and says, with a smirk on his face, "I can."

"Okay, what do you have?" asked Mr. Cameron.

Biggy looked straight at me.

"Nat," he said, almost spitting it out as he scrawled 'N-A-T' in huge capitals across the board. "Nat," he repeated, plunking the chalk down and making his way back to his seat, still smirking at me. "You know," he said to the whole class, "Nat, as in a little bug!" At that, he snickered, while his buddies laughed out loud.

I suppose he wanted the name to stick, and maybe it would have. But what happened next shut him up real good.

I could tell that Mr. Cameron didn't like what Biggy did, and I figured that he would probably talk to Biggy while we were doing the reading assignment. So, just before we are about to read, Mr. Cameron says, "Any other questions or comments before we start the reading assignment?"

Marlene, who, by now, I knew, was the one Biggy really wanted to impress, raised her hand.

Everybody's looking in her direction, because, in the first place, nobody had ever heard her say anything in class. And in the second place--and I hate to admit this--she looked really cute.

"Marlene?" Mr. Cameron said, sounding kinda' surprised.

"Mr. Cameron, do you mind if I add something to the list?" she asks.

"Please . . ." Mr. Cameron said, getting up and handing her a piece of chalk.

With that, Marlene walks right to the front, and she turns and faces the class.

"Actually," she says, to nobody in particular, "I like the name Nat. It's a great nickname, because it describes something fast, something you can hardly see, and something that can totally bug you Sometimes a gnat can bug you so much you can't even concentrate. Before you know it, it's there. And before you know it, it's gone."

Did you ever have one of those times in your life that you'd like to just stay in, forever? This was one of those times. But it got even better. After saying what I just told you about, Marlene goes to the board, and writes a huge 'G' in front of the 'N-A-T.' Then she turns, looks straight at Biggy, and says, "Oh, by the way, I know this isn't Grade One. But you might like to learn this, anyway. The kind of gnat you were talking about is spelled 'G-N-A-T.' The 'G' stays silent."

That would have been bad enough for Biggy, but Marlene had one more thing to say. Right after she says, "The 'G' stays silent," she looks right at Biggy and says, "You might try that yourself sometime."

And then she goes to her desk and sits down.

I guess I'm not the only one who turns red at awkward times. Biggy turns three shades of red, and the whole class roars with laughter. Even Mr. Cameron had to turn his face away from the class. He pretended to erase the board. But from where I was sitting, I could see him laughing to himself.

I would have loved every second of this whole deal, except for one thing. In the back of my mind, I can hear Mr. Tunn, at Faith Christian School in Cheyenne, in one of our lessons on Proverbs. "He who digs a pit for another will end up falling into it himself," Mr. Tunn said after we had a discussion about what God says about getting even with people who hurt you. Well, King Solomon sure knew what he was talking about, because Biggy had tried to dig a pit for me. Not only did he fall into it himself. He was slam-dunked into it! By the exact person he was showing off for!

I was sure that, after all this, I'd see those eyes looking at me again. But Marlene buried herself in the reading assignment for the rest of the period. When she didn't look over at me, I could hardly wait for the end of the period. For sure, I thought, she'll be standing in the doorway again, and I was going to be ready with a cool smile. So at the end of the period, I tried the same thing as last time. I sorta' poked around, getting my things together, getting ready for the Big Moment when I would look up and see those eyes looking at me from the doorway. Out of the corner of my eye, I could see somebody standing in the doorway. By now, my heart is beating like a bongo drum, but it was now or never. I put on the best smile I had, and looked up.

It was Ned!

No wonder everybody called him 'Nerd!'

He was waiting to talk to me about some stupid thing or other--I can't even remember what. Why he decided to stand in the doorway, I have no idea. Probably that's why Marlene didn't stick around. Still, she didn't look at me before class ended. So maybe she just left because she had no reason to stay. Maybe I just imagined those eyes looking at me last time.

Now I was really mixed up!

I wondered how Marlene would act the next time in class.

## Chapter Eight: Trouble for Our Team

There was another reason I didn't really enjoy it as much as I could have when Biggy fell into the pit. I knew he was really mad. And I knew that he would try to think of some way to get even. I wasn't too worried about class, because the only class we had together was Mr. Cameron's. I was sure he wouldn't risk being faced again in front of Marlene. I wasn't worried about lunch time or dismissal time, either, because we had different schedules. Still, I was kind of on guard, because I knew Biggy wouldn't give up. There were a lot of kids who tried to hang around him. Any one of those kids could cause problems for me. Some of the kids who tried to hang around Biggy were in some other classes with me, so I was always expecting some trouble or other. Especially after what happened to Demski in Miss

MacIntyre's geometry class. After that, I tried to be ready for anything. Here's what happened.

Miss MacIntyre taught two classes: French and geometry. For some reason, she seemed to think it was cool to try to mix each subject together. Even if you weren't in her French class, you'd get something about France in geometry class. And if you weren't in her geometry class, for sure you'd get something about geometry in French class. I think she was trying to show her students that all subjects were related. Like that was something you had to tell somebody. I think you'd have to be a total idiot not to know that, but for some reason she had to keep hitting it over and over, until kids actually imitated her, and made it into a joke.

Another thing that was a joke was this model Eiffel Tower that Miss MacIntyre had on her reading table. Some kid who had been her pet a few years before had made it for her. It was made out of glued-together toothpicks and drinking straws. The kid was probably some dummy who was trying to get extra points. On the bottom of the tower was a card. The kid had printed on it. It said, "Eiffel Tower. Paris, France. Famous

Landmark." Underneath that, it said, "Geometry was important in building the Eiffel Tower."

"Duh-uh." (The "duh-uh" is me, not the card.) As dumb as it was, Miss MacIntyre loved it. The kid who made it was smart. He knew she would go for something about geometry connected to something about a French landmark. To her, it was a wonderful example of student interest, but to all of the kids it was a big joke. They called it the "Awful Tower," instead of the "Eiffel Tower," and kids would act like they were bowing to it and stuff when they came into class. Not in front of her, of course.

Well, this one day, Miss MacIntyre is giving us a quiz on the geography and history of France. She says a student's name, and then she asks a question. Not like Mr. Cameron, who asks a question, and then, like a tank commander, aims at you with his fifty millimeter finger. She kind of uses a slow singsong voice. It can make you want to go to sleep. And she goes around the room, one person after the other, up and down the rows, so that you practically could go to sleep if you count how many kids are ahead of you. Which is what Demski probably did. At least, he was in a faraway fog when Miss MacIntyre got to him. She knew he wasn't the brain of the class, so she tries to give him an easy question, and she says, "Mr. Demski? "The name of a famous tower in Paris."

I don't know where Demski's brain was. I know he wasn't what you'd call a super smart kid, but he wasn't as dumb as his answer was. Demski kind of looks like he walked in on a surprise party, and he blurts out, "The Tower of London?"

For a second, there's dead silence. Then everybody is cracking up. I don't make fun of people, but I'm telling you, this time I couldn't help laughing along with everybody else. "A famous tower in Paris." And Demski says, "The Tower of London!"

I don't know how long the laughing would have gone on if Miss McIntyre hadn't stopped it right away. She slams her hand on her desk, and says, "I do not find this amusing!" Then she goes on and on about people who don't pay attention, and it doesn't seem to matter how hard she works, and a bunch of other stuff, but I don't think anybody heard a word of it. You could hear kids snickering and you didn't even want to look up, because you knew you'd bust out laughing. That was something you definitely did not want to do when Miss MacIntyre was not happy!

I did manage to sneak a peak at Demski. I know he didn't hear the question, because he's no honor roll student, but he's not that dumb. Besides, he was sitting there looking like he wondered what was coming off. I felt sorry for him.

Miss MacIntyre's so mad that she stomps out of the room, and she no sooner hits the hallway when some of Biggy's friends start into a chant:
"Dumb-ski, Dumb-ski, thinks with his rump-ski!"

I already told you about how mad Demski gets. Well, Miss MacIntyre wasn't out of the room for more than maybe ten seconds when the chanting started. That's all the time it took for Demski to blow up. All the next stuff happened at once. Demski grabs his French book, turns in his desk, and fires it at Biggy's buddies. Of course, he's so furious, he misses. And of course, what do you think he hits? The Awful Tower. Just at the very second that Miss MacIntyre walks back into the room.

I can't describe the look on her face. It was like the worst look you've ever seen on a late night horror movie on television.

Demski's book goes sailing right into the reading table, and the Awful Tower becomes an mangled mess of busted toothpicks and twisted drinking straws.

What she did next must have made Miss MacIntyre feel terrible, because she had been trying to help Demski think he was smart. That was the reason for her easy question about the Eiffel Tower in Paris. But now, with her Awful Tower lying there in pieces, she screams something in French. *"Franchement tu es nul! Comment est-ce tu peux viens dans MON cours et faites le connerie comme-ca? Tu es fou ou quoi?"* That's what we figured out from the French-English dictionary.

Of course, at that particular moment, what she said didn't mean a thing to us. For one thing, it came out about ten times faster than when she was teaching vocabulary in French. For another thing, we had never heard any of the words before. But you never in your life saw such a scramble for the French-English dictionaries. So whether she wanted to or not, for the first time all year, Miss MacIntyre suddenly got everybody super interested in French. Even Demski. Which was too bad, because, when she lost her cool and screamed all that stuff, we found out later that what she said was something like, *"Seriously, you're stupid! How can you come into MY class like this and act like such an idiot? Are you nuts, or what?"* But we didn't know what she was saying at the time.

Without even taking a breath, she suddenly switches to English, and hollers at Demski, "YOU will report to me after class, and WE will arrange for Saturday detention!"

Suddenly, I felt like I had fallen off the top of the real Eiffel Tower. Saturday detentions took place on the first Saturday of the month. The championship game was on the first Saturday of the month--two weeks away! The game would start at ten in the morning, and Demski would be in detention until ten in the morning! He would never make it on time for the game. And without Demski, we were sunk! The Warriors would annihilate us.

I knew Demski had a temper, but I thought he had at least some self-control. I was wrong. He looks at Miss MacIntyre and blurts out, "That's what *you* say! I won't be there!"

"OUT!" she hollers, and points at the door. That meant, for sure, that Demski was on his way to the principal's office.

I guess by then Demski knew he was up to his crotch in crocodiles, because he kept his mouth shut and followed orders. I felt like I was watching the championship walk out the door with him.

There had to be some way to get us out of this jam!

# Chapter Nine: The Trouble Gets Worse

Championship game or not, there was no way Demski was going to get out of detention. Coach Arnold had even called the school and tried to talk the principal into letting Demski serve detention the following month, instead of on the day of the championship game. "If I bend the rules for one person, I have to bend them for everybody," was the principal's answer. So whichever way you wanted to look at it, the best we could hope for was that we could maybe stall in our warmups, and slow things down during the game. That way, maybe Demski could at least get out in time to get to the game halfway through the Second Period or something.

You could tell that Demski felt terrible about losing his temper, but it was too late. The detention wouldn't have been a big deal to him, but being late for the game was another thing. Even Demski knew that he was the glue that held the team together. So when you'd see Demski anywhere, he wouldn't look at anybody. He had kind of a permanent dead look on his face, like he wasn't really inside his body. The only thing you could think of was that he was still mad. And that he would stay that way. I felt sorry for him, but I knew that his bad attitude would create trouble. The problem was, it created trouble for me, not Demski.

Everybody knew that we were on the same team. They probably thought that we hung out together after school, too. But that part was not true. I liked Demski, and I was glad we had him for our goalie. But I wouldn't have hung out with him. Back at Cheyenne, I remembered Mr. Tunn telling about some kid who was sent to prison because a guy he had hung out with had shot somebody. The kid who went to prison was out in his buddy's car, and wasn't even in the fast food store where the guy got shot. But he went to prison anyway. Mr. Tunn told us about that when he was teaching us a couple of other proverbs from Solomon. One of them warned against hanging around with somebody who has a bad temper. The other proverb had something to do with good people being ruined by bad friends. Not that Demski was a bad kid. But he did have a bad temper. That was enough to make me think of the proverb. So I didn't hang out with him.

But that didn't matter. I still got into trouble because of Demski, but not really because of Demski. That sounds crazy, but what happened was that Miss MacIntyre's car got tagged in the parking lot with blaze orange spray paint. There was a bad word, in big letters, from the back of the car to the front of the car. It was splotched on, like it was done in a hurry, but you could make out what the word was. Somebody could have easily done it without being seen. All they had to do was walk through the parking lot, hold a small spray can next to their pocket, and spray while they were walking between parked cars. It didn't take much to ruin the paint. And it cost a lot to fix.

Whoever did the paint job had plans for getting me into trouble. The same morning that Miss MacIntyre's car got keyed, somebody left a note on her desk. It said, *"For making Demski do detention, there's a special favour waiting for you on your car."* Naturally, she was curious, so she heads out to the parking lot the first chance she gets. Of course, I don't know anything about any of this at the time, so I don't have any idea what is going on when I see Miss MacIntyre actually running toward the principal's office, looking like she's going to bawl. I didn't think too much of it then, but I sure did about fifteen minutes later.

We were sitting in Mr. Cameron's class, working on some map work we were supposed to do. We were supposed to put colored logos of professional teams next to the cities the teams were from. I had just pulled out my notebook to get started when Ned pokes me. He's leaning across the aisle from behind me, and he hands me a note, all folded up, with "Demski" in large letters on it, and makes like I'm supposed to pass it on to Demski. Between Demski and me is this kid--I don't even know his name--who always sits in the back with Biggy and his crowd. For some reason, today he's in the seat across from me, and sort of ahead of me. Well, I lean over and tap him on the shoulder, and go to hand him the note, pointing at Demski.

Well, as he reaches out to take it, he starts making enough fuss to get Mr. Cameron to look up. Then he pulls his hand away, and the note falls on the floor. So there I am, looking like I'm creating a problem.

"Mr. Metcalf," Mr. Cameron says. "Would you retrieve your mail and bring it up here, please."

"But I . . . " I started to say.

The kid I tried to hand it to bends over and picks it up, and makes like he wants to hand it back to me. But I suddenly knew it meant more trouble for me than just passing a note. That wouldn't have been too much of a problem. But I had the funny feeling that there was more going on here than I thought. So like a dummy, when the kid handed it back, I kept my hands at my sides, and let the note fall to the floor.

"Mr. Metcalf, I'm not going to ask you again!"

I felt hot, and I could feel my neck and cheeks getting red. By now, everybody was staring, and it was deadly quiet. Mr. Cameron was a good guy, and a good teacher, but there was one thing you didn't do in his class, and that was break the rules. If he gave you some seatwork to do, you did it. No talking. No notes. No daydreaming. Still, other than the strange feeling I had that something really bad was about to happen, I figured that the person who wrote the note was the one who was really in trouble. Once Mr. Cameron opened it and found out who wrote it, he'd know that I was just passing it on. So I picked it up, shuffled to the back of the room, handed it to him, and turned to go back to my seat.

I had gone about four steps, when suddenly I hear, "METCALF!" I felt like an elk smacked by a 180 grain slug.

"Metcalf!"

Now the room was as quiet as a tomb. Nobody's even writing.

Mr. Cameron has this look on his face like one of the French Revolution guillotine guys we had read about in Miss MacIntyre's French class. Without another word, he swings his head toward the door, and there was no mistaking what he meant.

I never realized, before that moment, how big Mr. Cameron was. I felt like I was a criminal and he was the warden of some prison. Before I could even move, his hand was on my elbow, and I was being propelled from the room.

I was probably more confused than scared. But I was soon to get more scared. Mr. Cameron marched me straight down to the office. When we got there, he pointed at one of the deep leather chairs in the waiting room, and he headed right into the principal's room. Through the glass doors, I can see him showing the principal the open note. They both look out at me, and then the principal picks up the phone. He's on the phone for about a minute, and then he strides toward the glass door, swings it open, points at me to come in, and says, "Now!" Like it's time for me to get my head chopped off on the guillotine. You can guess how scared I was by now. Like I said, I can handle almost anything, even bad stuff, if I know what to expect. But there was no way to figure out what to expect.

On the principal's desk was the note. It was open. I couldn't see what it said. But even though it was upside down, there was no mistaking the name at the bottom. There, in large letters, surrounded by a design of two crossed hockey sticks with a puck in between, was the name of the person who had sent the note.

NATE.

And what the note said, I was to discover, would bring me trouble that could not only keep me out of the championship game. It could get me kicked off the team

and expelled from school!  Or, as I was to
find out later, maybe even worse!

# Chapter Ten: Guilty, With No Way Out

The vandalism to Miss MacIntyre's car was serious business. It would cost a lot of money to fix, and a report had been filed with the police. I found out later that when the principal had picked up the phone, he was calling the police. While I was standing in his office, he made another call.

It was to my Dad.

The principal was facing the window, and talking on the phone. He turned for a moment, and he was saying, " . . . some serious trouble, here, Mr. Metcalf, and I think you should see it for yourself." That's the only thing I heard before he turned back to the window. Then he's listening to something, and the next thing I hear is, "That's correct. Vandalism. And we have the evidence to prove it. No, Mr. Metcalf, I'm not mistaken. Your son *is* Nathan, isn't

that correct? Well, we practically caught him red-handed. We're going to file a police report, and we'll have to have you pick him up.
He is suspended from school until further notice."

You can probably guess that I was beyond scared by now. I still had no idea what was in the note. All I knew was that my name was on it, and that it was somehow connected to Miss MacIntyre's car. Through the window, I could see a police car pull into the parking lot. Two officers got out and headed toward the main entrance to the school. Out of the corner of my eye, I could tell that the secretary was waving her hands around, talking to somebody, and it looked like Miss McIntyre. I didn't dare turn my head to make sure. I tried to pray, but I couldn't even think of what to say. But then, all of a sudden, I start thinking of a verse we learned at Awana. *"Fear thou not, for I am with thee; be not afraid, for I am thy God."* That was the first moment my heart stopped pounding since Mr. Cameron had hauled me out of class. I could hardly breathe. If they thought I sprayed Miss MacIntyre's car, I might get sent to juvenile court. A judge could send me to Reform School. Even if I didn't get sent to Reform School, I could get expelled. I'd have to be taught at home. They would send a home-bound teacher, and keep me away from other kids. No matter what they decided, one thing was certain. I would not be able to play hockey. If you were in trouble with the police, you were kicked out of the league. All my dreams of playing in the championship game and being picked for Development Camp would be over.

One thing I didn't want to do was cry. I felt like it. I just tried to stand there with a "stone face," which is what I do when I get into trouble. But this was more trouble than I had ever been in, in my life. I was biting the side of my tongue, just to keep control of myself.

How much longer I could have kept it up, I don't know. Here are all these people standing around--Mr. Cameron, the principal, the secretary, two policemen, and whoever it was that the secretary had been talking to, and here's me in the middle of them.

Just when I figured I was going to lose it, I hear the secretary saying, "Right this way, Mr. Metcalf." Finally, I turned my head toward the outer office. My Dad was striding into the room, and he was looking straight at me, like I was the only one there.

You'd think that I wouldn't want my Dad there, right? Well, it was exactly the opposite. All of a sudden I felt real calm. I didn't know what was going to happen. But I knew one thing for sure. My Dad did not jump to conclusions. One thing he had taught us kids, over and over, was that we should always make sure we hear all sides of a story. More than once, I heard him say, when he and Mom were discussing something that was on the news, or in the paper, was "He who answers a matter before hearing the whole of it, is a fool." So he never made up his mind about anything until he heard the whole story. I knew I would get the chance to tell him my side of the story.

"We're going to have to send Nathan home with you today," the principal was saying. "We called you today because this type of thing is a more serious problem than simply breaking the school rules. As I told you on the telephone, the damage to Miss MacIntyre's car is considerable. The insurance company directed us to file a damage report. And, of course, along with that, we are required, by law, to contact the police.  These officers have with them a written report from Miss MacIntyre.  We'll need to have you read it over and sign it to indicate that you've been provided with a copy.  We will also give you a copy of the report," he said, handing Dad a sheet of paper covered with writing.

"And the note?" Dad said, pointing to the paper with my name on it on the principal's desk.

"Yes, we'll provide a copy of the note, too," the principal replied, handing the note to the secretary, who was still standing there.  "You understand that we'll have to keep the original."

"I understand," Dad replied, nodding his head, and acting perfectly calm.
By this time, he was standing next to me, with his hand on my shoulder.

"I'm going to have to be honest with you, sir," Dad continued.  "I realize that you had to call me to school.  I also realize that you had to call the police.  But there's one thing that bothers me, here, and I think I need to be direct with you."

Mr. Stelvin--that's the principal-- suddenly looked uncomfortable.  He swallowed hard, but before he could say anything, Dad continued. "If Nathan is found to be responsible for what happened, he will accept the consequences, and I will also deal with this at home. HOWEVER," Dad continued, with the "however" coming out the way it always did when Dad wanted to make people think, "I am *very* concerned by the fact that it seems that everyone has decided that Nathan is guilty, without even allowing Nathan to speak for himself."

Dad looked down at me. "Nathan," he said, "The handwriting on the note looks like your handwriting. The paper the note is written on looks like it was torn out of your notebook. You were the one passing the note."

By now, the secretary is back in the room, and she hands the note to Mr. Stelvin, and the copy to Dad.

Dad reads the note again, and then looks at Mr. Stelvin, and says, "Sir, again, I have to be completely honest with you. This note does not sound like my son. It looks like his handwriting, and it looks like his notebook paper, but it does not sound like anything Nathan would ever do."

You could tell that Mr. Stelvin thought that Dad was acting like a parent who could never think his kid would do anything wrong. There are lots of parents like that.

Some of them have really bad kids. But they can never believe that their kids could get into trouble. So he kind of sighs, and sits down. For a few seconds, he doesn't say anything. Then he looks at Dad, and says, "I think we all need time to think this over. Mr. Metcalf, what we'll do today is send Nathan home with you. No doubt some of the students saw these two officers drive up. And, of course, they know that Mr. Cameron escorted Nathan out of class. For Nathan's benefit, I think he should go with you for the time being." Looking at the secretary, Mr. Cameron, and the officers, Mr. Stelvin then said, "We'll keep this whole incident quiet for now. We will investigate the matter further. Until then, Nathan may attend class," he said, looking directly at Mr.Cameron, "and we will keep things as normal for him as possible."

"One more thing," Mr. Stelvin said. "Mr. Metcalf, you're right in saying that we have not allowed Nathan to speak for himself. With your permission, I'd like to give him that opportunity before we all leave this office."

Dad nodded, looking at me.

"Son, what would you like to say for yourself?" Mr. Stelvin said. He sounded a lot calmer now than he had sounded when I first came into the room.

The words came flying out of me and I almost lost my breath. "That's not my note I didn't start to pass it somebody gave it to me the only thing I know is that it was for Demski and the kid I passed it to held out his hand and pulled it away and I don't even know what's in it!"

One of the officers stepped forward and picked up the note. He stared at it. He had a strange look on his face. He was talking to me, but he was looking right at Mr. Stelvin. "You-don't-even-know-what's-IN-it?!" he said, very slowly, and making each word sound like it was squeezed out of an empty plastic ketchup bottle. He was still looking at Mr. Stelvin.

Mr. Stelvin swallowed again. But this time nobody said anything.

Now Dad looked straight at Mr. Stelvin and Mr. Cameron. All of a sudden, I felt a little bit sorry for Mr. Cameron. But not too sorry for Mr. Stelvin.

"You mean, Nathan has not been given an opportunity to look at the note he is alleged to have passed?" Dad said. This time, his voice did not sound quite as reasonable as it had before.

Mr. Stelvin and Mr. Cameron each got a funny look on their face. They kind of looked at each other, and then Mr. Cameron reached over and picked the note up. He took two steps, and handed it to me.

I think I did the fastest speed reading that had ever been done in the world.

No wonder I was in so much trouble!

It was going to take a miracle to get me out of this.

## Chapter Eleven: Nerd Starts a Miracle

I was still pretty shook up by the time we got to the car. With only Dad there, I lost it. Before we even went a half a block, I started to cry.

"Nate," Dad said, reaching over and squeezing my shoulder, "don't worry about this. There is no way on earth you would write such a note. And there's no way on earth that you would do what the note said. I believe in you. We'll solve this, one way or another."

By this time I was crying pretty hard. You would, too, I bet. Because when Mr. Cameron handed me the note, it really did look like my handwriting. And it sure looked like I was guilty. It said,

*"Hey, Demski. I just got even for us. Every time MacIntyre sees the new colour*

*on her car, she'll think about what she did to you."* And then, of course, there was my name, with the two crossed hockey sticks and a puck. *"NATE."*

"But how can I prove it?" I cried. "It really does look like my handwriting. And it's on my notebook paper. And everybody knows that Demski's detention will hurt our team! I probably won't get to play in the championship!" and I started bawling even more.

"Nate," Dad said, "This doesn't make any sense. But remember, the Lord is still in charge of everything that happens to you. Jesus said that not one hair can fall from your head without your Heavenly Father's permission. Remember what God says. 'All things work together for good to them that love God.'"

Dad sure knew how to calm a guy down. "Okay," I thought. "I'll ask the Lord to help me. If God wants me to play, He will let me play. If He doesn't want me to play, for some reason I don't understand, then He will keep me from playing." But I have to admit, every prayer I said was that God would let me play.

Mom came out into the driveway before we even pulled into the yard. She was

71

trying to smile, but I could see that she was upset. She looked at Dad, then at me, and then at Dad again. Her face seemed to say, "Well . . .?"

Dad went through the whole story, from the part about the spray paint on the car, the insurance company, the note, the police, and the meeting in Mr. Stelvin's office. He repeated the part about what he had said to me--about how the Lord was in charge, and how we would be fine, regardless of what might happen. The only part he left out was my crying in the car. I was glad he did. The one time Mom had seen me cry since I was a little kid was the day we turned north on Highway 85, heading out of Cheyenne toward Manitoba. A big bomber on a training run from the base flew right over our car, real low. The men in Dad's squadron knew when we were leaving, and they timed it just right. When we got out on the highway, they did a fly-by and dipped the plane's wing to say goodbye. I think that's when I realized that I probably wouldn't see my friends at Faith Christian ever again--until heaven, that is. That made me get tears in my eyes. Well, Mom had seen the tears, and she felt so bad for me that she burst into tears herself. So I was glad

Dad didn't say anything about my crying. Mom always got very upset when any of her kids got hurt, or when their feelings got hurt.

After Dad got finished with the story, Mom immediately jumped up and said, "Nathan, you must be hungry. You've missed your lunch and you need to eat," and with that, she headed to the kitchen.

After all that had happened, I wasn't hungry, but I didn't say anything. I knew that Mom and Dad wanted to talk some more. So I headed for my room to put my stuff away. Besides, I needed to think. By this time, my head had started to hurt, so I thought I'd stretch out on the bed for a couple of minutes. I buried my face in the pillow and started to think things over.

Who could have sprayed Miss MacIntyre's car? Who could have torn a page from my notebook? Who would be able to copy my handwriting exactly? In fact, who could have even gotten hold of anything with my handwriting on it? Questions were flying through my head like geese in a snowstorm.

"Nate!" "Nate!" It was Mom. And she was knocking at my bedroom door. In Manitoba, it gets dark in the winter at about four o'clock, and when I sat up, I could see that it was already late afternoon. I had dozed off! It was almost time for practice! Thank goodness Mom kept track of this stuff! I could always depend on her. It took me about two seconds to jump out of bed and start grabbing my gear. I was feeling really pumped. Then everything came rushing back, and I got kind of a sick feeling in my gut.

It must have shown on my face, because when I walked into the kitchen, the first thing Mom said was, "Nate, are you ok? Are you sick?"

One thing is, I don't lie to my parents. So I said, "No, Mom. I'm not sick." I wasn't lying. I wasn't really sick. I just felt sick. I felt like I had a bad stomach ache. But there was no way I was going to tell my folks. They would have grilled me for half an hour. Dad would have done a Coach Arnold number on me, and said something like, "When the going gets tough, the tough get going." Mom would have insisted that I go to the doctor. Her brother, my Uncle Keith, had played in a game with an inflamed appendix when he was a kid. It burst, and he had to have an emergency operation. Ever since, Dad would tease Mom, and tell her she was --what did he call it?-- 'paraphrased' or 'paranoid' or something like that. Ned would have known. Whatever the word was, it meant being a worry wart. Those are all the reasons I said I wasn't sick. But I sure felt sick.

I managed to head off to practice without eating. Even though Mom had tried to get me to "at least have a snack," I kept thinking of starts and stops and puking over the boards. I finally promised her I'd have a huge bedtime feast, so she let me go. Mom had a way of knowing when to get on my case and when it was better to give me slack..

Practice was good and bad at the same time. It was good because it made my stomachache go away, and it made all that stuff at school go away. It was bad, because Coach Arnold was driving us like a squad of commandos about to go on a suicide mission. Except that he wanted the commandos to go on the mission and return alive. That would have been fine, but I felt like practice was going to kill me!

One way this practice was different was that Billy Benton was in goal for most of the practice. Coach Arnold knew that, at best, Demski might make it to the arena in time for the third period. At worst, he wouldn't get there at all. Of course, Demski was still hoping that by some stroke of luck he was going to get out of detention. He was hoping his mom would go to school and argue his case, but she wouldn't do it. "In the long run," Mrs. Demski told Coach Arnold, "this might do more good for my son than playing in a championship game ever would."

Well, Mrs. Demski might have been right. Mom thought she was. "Now there's a woman I can respect," Mom declared. "Somebody who actually knows what's important and sticks to it!" I hadn't thought about it that way until that moment, but I had often heard adults talking about parents who wouldn't discipline their kids. Mom was probably right, as far as what was good for Demski. Maybe it actually would do Demski more good to miss a game than winning a championship would. But I couldn't help thinking, "What about the rest of us?" And I wondered what Demski's dad would think. I was sure that he hadn't heard about all the trouble Demski was in. Demski's parents were divorced, and his dad lived in Vancouver. Even though he was that far away, he still caught a couple of games when his job brought him to Manitoba. I was sure Mr. Demski wouldn't go for this detention-miss-the-championship-game stuff!

I was also sure Coach Arnold was thinking about all this, too. Maybe he was driving us so hard because he knew that, without Demski, we were going to have a hard time of it. Everybody on the team knew that it was Demski who had kept us in most of the games. It was Demski who never gave up. And it was Demski who had turned away fifty-two shots by the Warriors in that last game that had brought us to the playoffs.

Coach Arnold played it totally straight with us. "Boys," he said seriously, "we all know that superior goaltending is what kept us in a lot of games. We all hoped that Demski would be able to be in goal for the whole game. It doesn't look like that's gonna' happen right now. But I don't want you to forget that we got to the championship as a team. Not as individuals. A team. It was a team that beat the Warriors. It will be a team that will win the championship. It will be very important for you to do exactly as I tell you to do. Don't count on any one man to do something spectacular and win the game. Think as a team. Think as a unit. Each one of you do what you are supposed to do. Don't worry about the other guy and what he's supposed to do. Worry about yourself. Do your job to the best of your ability, and you'll skate away as champions!"

So Coach Arnold hadn't heard about my problem yet. Or maybe he had.
Maybe that was the reason for all his "Play as a team," warnings. Then, too, near the end of practice, I heard Coach Arnold telling Demski, "Keep practicing as hard as you can. How you practice is how you'll play. Put out a hundred per cent in practice, and you'll put out a hundred per cent in the game. Be sloppy in practice, you'll be sloppy in the game." Then, for some reason, Coach glanced at me and seemed to talk to both Demski and me. "The only thing in life that you have control over is yourself."

I did put out a hundred per cent. Maybe more. By the time practice was over, I was totally whipped. I didn't feel like talking to anybody. But I had to. Dad was in the car, waiting to pick me up. And there was a kid in the car with him. It was Ned. What on earth was Ned doing there?

Before I could even ask why he was there, Dad reached over and handed me a paper plate piled high with pizza. "Nate," he said, "Your Mom knew you'd be starving. Have at it! There's a lot more waiting for you when we get home." Dad had a grin on his face that told me that something better than pizza was coming. "I think you'll listen better to what Ned has to say if your stomach isn't growling while you listen."

Ned began to talk. Nonstop. But it was okay. Because I didn't want to stop him.

He knew who did the "Demski" thing, he confided! He had proof. First, he had been in the restroom, in one of the stalls, he said, when he had overheard some kids talking. Yes, he admitted, it sounded like something stupid from a movie--overhearing a people talking in the washroom. But that was exactly what happened, he insisted. They were talking about a kid called "Stick," of all things. He was kind of a manager for the Warriors. His main job was looking after the team's hockey sticks. Nobody paid too much attention to him, even though he was always trying to do things that would make the kids on the Warriors team think he was cool. Anyway, this "Stick" kid was the one who sprayed Miss MacIntyre's car. Ned also heard them talking about what was in the note to Demski! Ned figured that "Stick" was also the kid who probably wrote the notes. How he figured that out, I would have to wait to find out, because by then, we were at his house, and we had to drop him off. Since it was dark, Dad went to the door of his house with him. Ned's Dad waved to me to come in.

"I understand your son's situation," Ned's Dad was telling my Dad, as we stood in the hallway of Ned's house. "The problem is, if a gang of kids finds out that Ned was the one who found out who did the spray job, he'll be in danger. Actually," Ned's Dad said, "the danger Ned will be in will be just as serious as the problems Nate is facing. Kids who would spray paint a car and write notes to get your son into trouble sound like pretty mean kids to me. They might find a way to pick on Ned. I don't know how you're going to do it, but you'll have to prove who did it without identifying Ned as your source of information."

"That will be almost impossible," Dad replied. "There's no way to prove what Ned overheard, unless Ned comes forward. But I agree with you. That would be dangerous for Ned. We won't put him in that predicament. It wouldn't be fair to him. In any case," Dad said, shaking hands with Ned's father, "I do thank you for telephoning me, and for letting Ned come with me to the rink. We'll have to figure out how to get to the truth without revealing how we found out."

About that time, Ned, who is standing there saying nothing, suddenly pops up and exclaims, "Wait! There's one more thing!"

Ned's mother, who had been standing in the kitchen, listening to everything, called out. "For goodness sake, dear, let's get to the bottom of this. Mr. Metcalf, Nate, take off your coats. I've got some hot chocolate here that'll take just a minute or two to prepare. Come on and sit down and let's think through this together."

A few minutes later, we were in Ned's parents' family room, sipping hot chocolate. There was no light in the room except for the light from the fire in the fireplace, which Ned's Dad had piled high with poplar logs. Ned looked almost like some weird character in a detective story as the light and shadows from the fire flickered back and forth across his face.

"There's one more thing," Ned said, when we had all settled down in the darkened room. "It just hit me when we were standing in the hallway," he continued. "There's one thing that kid, "Stick," can do better than anybody else. He can draw," he said. Looking at me, Ned asked, "Did you ever notice that he's always drawing hockey players and stuff on his buddies' notebooks? Did you ever notice that he's the one who does the lettering on their locker cards?" Talking faster now, Ned continued, "And did you ever notice that he's left-handed?"

I was glad that neither my Dad nor Ned's parents knew why that was important, either. Because I sure didn't. Ned waited, as though he expected all of us to get excited. But nobody got it. So we just waited. His parents were looking at him as though they were used to this. There was no question about it. Ned was a brain.

"Think about it," Ned explained. "'Stick' wants to get in good with the guys on the team. He wants them to think that he's important to the Warriors, too. But nobody thinks he is, because he's just a stickboy. So he wants to help them win the championship. How better to do that then to get Nathan out of the game? And how can he do that? By getting him into bad trouble. He already knows that Nathan isn't going to do anything stupid, like lose his temper. Or talk back to a teacher. So what does he do? He decides to spray Miss MacIntyre's car.

Why Miss MacIntyre? Because he can make it look like somebody who is a buddy of Demski's is getting even. And he has to make it serious enough to get the person kicked out of school, because he knows that if you get expelled, you're history. No more hockey. No playoffs, no nothing!"

Ned sat there, grinning with satisfaction, expecting that we would all see exactly what he was telling us. Trouble was, we didn't. So his mom says, "Go on, Ned, what's this business about left-handed and such?"

"Okay," Ned says, leaning forward, and really digging in. He was liking the attention, now, and really getting warmed up. "The guy who spray-painted the car is left-handed. The word he sprayed on the car is printed on the side of the car. It starts at the back of the car, and goes forward. The only way to spray something like that, in the parking lot, without being seen, is to hold the spray can low. Next to your pocket. You would have to keep walking, so that nobody would remember anybody hanging around any particular car. So you would have to spray while you are walking. That would be easy to do, left-handed or right handed. *Unless*," Ned continued, enjoying every minute of this, "Unless you wanted to write something. If you wanted to write something, you would use the hand you usually write with. The word was on the right side of the car. It started at the back of the car and went toward the front. It was at pocket height. It had to be done by a left-handed person holding the spray can low enough not to be seen."

Ned sat there with a satisfied smile, looking at all of us. The flames were still dancing in the fireplace, and I realized that I hadn't taken even one more sip of hot chocolate the whole time. Ned's Dad was the first to speak. He looked amused, even though this was serious business.

"Even if that is so, Ned, how will that be helpful? And how does that fit in with that boy--what's his name--and his ability as an artist?"

"Simple," Ned says, holding his hands out like some magician explaining an child's trick. "'Stick' is about the only kid who could take a sheet of Nate's notebook paper and write a note in handwriting that looks like Nate's writing. Nobody else is that good of an artist."

"That's pretty tough to prove, son," Ned's dad said, shaking his head. "Pretty tough."

By now, Ned was really enjoying this. The kid was really something. He was not only a brain. He was a genius. He sticks his finger in the air, and says, like some character in a mystery, "Aha! There is one sure way we can at least prove that Nate did not do it. That will at least get Nate out of trouble. And we will do it right in front of the whole class!"

By the time Dad and I got home, my head was spinning. I really didn't understand why I couldn't go straight to Mr. Stelvin and the police and tell them what Ned had heard. But Dad said that we absolutely could not do that. He even said it was in the Bible. "Solomon," Dad explained, "warned us not to use a friend's secret to argue our own case. Even if we win the case, if we harm the friend, it's not worth it."

It seemed worth it to me. I figured I had more to lose than Ned did.

Ned wouldn't tell anyone why his plan would work. He just kept saying, "If Mr. Cameron will go along with what I have in mind, it will prove that Nathan is not guilty. But to really prove it, I can't even tell Nathan what I have in mind."

All Ned would have to do would be to get Mr. Cameron to cooperate. He looked at his dad and said, "Dad, will you talk to Mr. Cameron for me? I think our chances will be better if you and Mr. Metcalf take my idea to him.
He'll believe you if you tell him that even Nathan doesn't know what the plan is.

Now I was really nervous. What if Ned's plan ended up making me look even more guilty? Then what? But I had to go along with it. I had no other way to prove that I was innocent, except to use a friend's secret. And I couldn't do that, after what Dad had said.

I could only trust in God and hope that Ned was as much of a super-nerd-brain as everybody said he was.

## Chapter Twelve: The Plan Works!

I wasn't wrong when I said that Mr. Cameron was a good guy. When Ned's dad and my dad told Mr. Cameron about Ned's plan, he rubbed his hands together and said, softly, "Hmmm. Well, I always try to keep an open mind. This is very unusual. But it's worth a try. Let me be the one to talk to Mr. Stelvin about this, and get his okay. I know he was embarrassed when the police officer confronted him about not even letting Nathan see the note Nathan was accused of writing. He's a reasonable man. He'll want to bend over backward to make sure Nathan is treated fairly. I'm sure he'll agree to this." Then he said, again. "This *is* unusual, though, gentlemen."

Ned and I could hear all of this, but we weren't a part of the conversation. We stayed out in the hallway, because our dads thought it would be better if there were no kids present when they first laid out the plan. We were straining to hear every word, and when we heard Mr. Cameron agreeing to the plan, Ned jumped up and high-fived me. He barely had time to sit back down before Mr. Cameron leaned through the doorway and waved to us to come in.

"Nathan," Mr. Cameron said, looking directly at me. "You understand why I had to march you out of the room the way I did the other day." It wasn't a question, it was more like a statement.

"Well, I'm not really sure," I answered. That was the truth. I wasn't sure. It wasn't like Mr. Cameron to act the way he did when he intercepted the note. I couldn't figure out why everything became so serious so fast when he called me to bring the note back to his desk.

"You know that I don't tolerate any fooling around," Mr. Cameron explained. "I had to get on your case immediately. If I had not done so, it would have set a bad example for everyone else. That's why I marched you out the way I did. It was nothing personal. I do think, though, that I owe you an apology. I don't know whether it was you wrote the note. Nor do I know whether Ned's plan will point to someone else. Nevertheless, whether you wrote the note or not, I should not have jumped to conclusions so quickly. That was my mistake. I hope you will forgive me."

"Of course Nathan will forgive you," Dad interrupted, before I could even answer. "We all make mistakes. The important thing to do is to get at the truth. Mr. Cameron, when can you put Ned's plan into action?"

"Why wait?" Mr. Cameron answered, looking first at Dad, and then at Ned's dad. "Assuming that Mr. Stelvin goes along with it, we'll do it the next time the boys are in class with me." Looking at his schedule, he continued, " . . .which will be tomorrow morning."

The men shook hands, and Dad started herding us toward the door. "Lord," I was praying silently, "Please let Ned's plan work. Please let the truth come out."

I don't have any clue about what any of my other classes were about for the rest of that afternoon. I don't remember much about practice that evening. I can't tell you what we had for supper. All I could think about was Mr. Cameron's class and Ned's plan. What if it didn't work? How could I possibly prove that I was innocent? I headed for bed as early as I could, not because I was tired, but just to get the night over with. Ned's plan just *had* to work, whatever it was! That was the last thought I had before I drifted off to sleep.

Everything that happened before Mr. Cameron's class seemed to go in slow motion. When the time finally came, I think I was the first person in the room. "Dumb!" I thought to myself. "If Mr. Cameron sees me in here first, he'll think I know what the plan is!" But I hardly had time to think about that when a bunch of other kids came in, so I was safe for the time being. I was so nervous, I didn't even notice when Marlene came in. I wondered whether anyone would be staring at me because of my forced march from the room. I had my head down, pretending to review my notes. I could kinda' see everything going on. But of course, I couldn't tell whether anyone was looking at me. Out of the corner of my eye I saw Mr. Cameron in the hallway, and then, almost at the same moment, he was in the room.

As usual, he started the lesson as he crossed the room, without so much as a "hello," or a "good morning," or anything.

"You will remember," Mr. Cameron said, as though he was completing a sentence from two class periods ago, "that we were talking about how professional teams sometimes got their names from history or geography. Your assignment was to read your history text and make some guesses about why certain teams have the names they do. Anybody come up with anything?"

Several hands shot up, and Mr. Cameron nodded. One kid said, "Philadelphia Seventy-sixers, from 1776, the signing of the Declaration of Independence, in Philadelphia."

"Good!" Mr. Cameron replied, with a big smile on his face. "Anybody else?"

More hands went up, and kids were coming up with a pile of names, but I didn't hear even one of them. What had happened? Had Mr. Cameron changed his mind? Had he decided not to go through with Ned's plan? This was just a regular class period! I looked over toward Ned, but he was acting like he was really into the lesson. I knew it! I shouldn't have counted on anyone else! Least of all Ned. Ned the Nerd! That was a good name for him, I thought.

"Let's move on," Mr. Cameron was saying. "Let's have a little fun, and find out who likes which team, and why." At least, I think that's what he said. The only reason I heard that much was because I heard him say my name.

"I need a couple of people up at the chalkboard, to keep track of things. Nate, catch," he said, throwing me a piece of chalk. I was so startled, I almost dropped it. That would have been bad news in front of this class!

A bunch of kids shot their hands in the air, acting like they wanted to be at the board. Mr. Cameron threw out a piece of chalk to two other kids. One of them was "Stick." "Oh, great," I thought, "by the time everybody talks about what team they like, and why they like them, that'll be the end of the period. If there was going to be any plan, it's too late now!"

"Okay, you kids up at the board, make a couple of columns. At the top of one column, write "Favorite team." At the top of the other column, write "Team Colors."

You had to hand it to Mr. Cameron. He knew how to get kids into a lesson. Everybody was really into this. Everybody except me, that is. I was still wondering why

Mr. Cameron had decided not to put Ned's plan into action.

But then things changed in a flash!

I had just finished writing the headings on top of the two columns. On the left, I wrote: *Favorite Team*. On the right, I wrote: *Team Colors*. The other kids at the board did the same. I had barely turned away from the board when Ned jumps up. I mean, actually jumps to his feet. He's pumping his hand up and down in the air, trying to get Mr. Cameron's attention, and pointing wildly at the board. All this time I'm wondering just exactly what is coming off. Mr. Cameron flashes Ned a look that told him that if he knew what was good for him, he'd sit down and shut his mouth. Which is what Ned did. Then Mr. Cameron says, looking at his watch, "Class, I think we'll continue this next time. We're about out of time, here, so you kids can visit for the few remaining minutes, and next time we'll take up where we left off."

Hardly ever did anyone get to spend any time just visiting in Mr. Cameron's class. Like I said, he didn't put up with any talking, note-passing, or loafing, and we usually had plenty of homework to get started on if there was any time left over at the end of a period.

So everybody was so glad not to have an assignment, that the talking started immediately, and nobody had a chance to even think about Ned's behavior. Besides, they were used to ignoring him. For once, that was a good thing for him.

Between the time everybody started visiting and the time the bell rang, Mr. Cameron gave Ned the high sign to stay after class. Everybody got up to leave, including me. I looked back at Ned, wondering what was going on.
Right behind Ned, standing at the back of the room, was Mr. Cameron, and he was giving me a look that said only one thing. "Stay after class."

Maybe Mr. Cameron was going to explain why he hadn't used Ned's plan.
Well, an explanation would help! I was really disappointed.

You could see that Ned could hardly contain himself. The last kid was barely out of the room when Ned blurts out "Look what Nate wrote! Look what Nate wrote!"

Believe me, at that point, I was really wondering what was going on, because I wrote down exactly what Mr. Cameron said to write. What had I done wrong this time?

Neither Ned nor Mr. Cameron noticed what was probably a real dumb look on my face. Mr. Cameron slapped Ned on the back and said, "Ned, you are probably the only kid in this school who could have figured out a way to prove Nate's innocence. But that's only half of the mystery. The other half is, how do we prove who really sprayed the car and wrote the notes?"

Don't get me wrong. I was thrilled that Mr. Cameron declared that I wasn't the person who wrote the notes. But I just didn't get what Ned and Mr. Cameron were talking about.

"I don't get it," I said, finally. "You mean you used Ned's plan? I thought you forgot to do it, or that you decided not to do it. What was it?
How do you know I'm not the one who wrote the note?"

"It's so simple, it would be a joke if it weren't so serious," Mr. Cameron laughed. "I'll let Ned explain."

Ned gets up and walks to the board. Now he looks like some kid scientist in a mystery movie. "Observe," he says, pointing to the headings that "Stick" and the other kid had written. "Observe how the other kids wrote "Favorite Team," and

"Team Colors." With his finger touching each letter, Ned says, "'F-a-v-o-u-r-i-t-e,'" and "'c-o-l-o-u-r-s.'" "Observe," he continues, sounding like some old man who had crawled into a kid's body, "that when you wrote those words, you spelled *favorite* and *colors* without the letter 'u'. That makes sense, because you used the American spelling. You've spent all your time in school in the United States. The other kids, of course, used the Canadian spelling. Remember what the notes to Miss MacIntyre said. One of the notes said"-- and by now, Nerd had picked up a piece of chalk--"'there's a special *favour* waiting for you,' and the other one," he said, "had something in it about a *colour*."

"Both of them used the Canadian spelling," Mr. Cameron added.

"I never even knew there was a difference!" I said, almost hollering..

"Precisely!" Ned exclaimed, still acting like a detective. "Everybody found out what was in the first note, because it was open on Miss MacIntyre's desk before she saw it. I knew that there would be a second note, and that it would have the word 'color' in it, somewhere, because of what I told you,

Nate. Remember, I told you how I found out?"

Mr. Cameron leaned forward with a serious look on his face. "What was that-- what did you tell Nate?"

"I prefer not to tell you, Sir," Ned answered. "Besides, how I found out won't really help prove who did it." Turning to me, Ned continued, "I noticed, right off, that your spelling was different. If you remember, I asked you for your notes on what the assignment was a few periods ago. Your notes said that we were supposed to design some team logos and color them. That's when I noticed that you spelled color without a 'u' in it. I didn't think anything of it, at the time, but it turned out to be a pretty important detail."

Mr. Cameron had a huge grin on his face by now. After all the kids he had to teach and all the work he had to do to get kids interested in school, I think he was really enjoying Ned's performance. I think he liked Ned's act as much as he liked Ned's brains.

"Ned," he said, still smiling, "too bad we had to keep this whole thing quiet. You put on quite a show. It's unfortunate that you didn't have an audience for this production!"

With that, Mr. Cameron headed for the door. Over his shoulder, he smiled at Ned and me and said, "Take it easy, guys. Nate, your worries about this incident are over." Then, joking, he says to Ned, "Detective, if you get any more ideas about how to find the real culprit, let me know."

I felt so good when Mr. Cameron said that my worries were over that I could have hollered at the top of my lungs! I figured that Ned would be grinning from ear to ear. But there he was, already thinking. Out loud.

"Hmmm," he said. "You and I and our dads know that 'Stick' is the guilty person. We already know that he could have written the notes, because of the way he spelled those words, and because he is a good artist. There have to be some clues to prove that he's guilty. I need to do some thinking."

We didn't say anything on the way out of class. We were both thinking. Hard. I was out of trouble. But it didn't seem right to let 'Stick' get away with this. Yet, I had to agree with Dad. As long as Ned didn't want anyone to know that he had overheard that conversation in the washroom, I would have to keep the information to myself.

There would have to be some other way to catch "Stick."

## Chapter Thirteen: 'Stick' Gets Stuck

I was glad that it wasn't up to me to have to prove that 'Stick' was the one who wrote the note. Thanks to Ned's plan, at least Mr. Stelvin, Mr. Cameron, and the police officers knew that I didn't do it! That was the main thing. Of course, everybody in class knew that I got into trouble for passing a note. They knew that I had to go to Mr. Stelvin's office. They also knew that the note was being passed to Demski. Even kids who were in some of my other classes had heard about it. What they didn't know was what was in the note. Only Mr. Stelvin, Mr. Cameron, the police officers, and my Dad and I knew what the note said. And, of course, 'Stick' knew what was in the note, because he wrote it. Exept that the only ones who knew that it was 'Stick' were Ned and me, and our dads.

I kept hoping that Ned would get up enough courage to go to Mr. Cameron and tell him that he had heard 'Stick' in the washroom, talking about writing a note. I kept hoping, but I didn't say anything to Ned. If he was scared to tell on 'Stick', I didn't blame him. If a kid was mean enough to spray paint a car and to try to put the blame on somebody else, it was hard telling what else he would do. Maybe he wouldn't have beaten Ned up. But he could have ruined his bike, or stolen stuff from his locker, or something worse. There was no way of knowing. So I really didn't expect Ned to come forward and tell what he had overheard.

Even though everything was scary at the time, one thing about the whole deal seems funny, now. I don't know how to explain it, but when I got into trouble for that note to Demski, every kid in my classes knew about it almost as soon as it happened. The funny part of it is what the kids said when I got out of trouble. Some kids had seen the police at the school. So a rumor started that Mr. Stelvin and Mr. Cameron called the police fingerprint squad to the school, and that the police said that my fingerprints weren't on the note. Ned and I thought that was really stupid. Of course my fingerprints were on the note. I was caught passing it! Nobody stops to think when they hear a rumor. They just repeat it.

I think that Ned felt bad about not telling Mr. Cameron about what he had heard in the washroom. All he talked about was how he could come up with a plan to show that 'Stick' was guilty. But Ned couldn't seem to think of anything that would work. As things turned out, he didn't have to.

There was one thing I couldn't figure out for a while. All of a sudden, 'Stick' started getting really friendly with me. When we did group work in Mr. Cameron's class, 'Stick' would come over to whatever group I was in. Whenever Mr. Cameron was watching or listening, 'Stick' would act especially friendly. It was really strange. I couldn't figure out what he was up to. Then Ned comes up to me between classes and says to me, "Why do you think 'Stick' is acting so friendly to you?"

"I've been wondering about that," I told Ned. "Maybe he feels sorry for what he did. Maybe he's trying to make it up to me."

But then Ned says to me, "Don't kid yourself. He's no dummy! He realizes that Mr. Cameron and Mr. Stelvin know that somebody was trying to get you into trouble. My guess is that he thinks that they'll be trying to figure out which kids don't like you. So he's putting on a big show."

I didn't want to believe Ned, at first. To tell you the truth, I felt sorry for 'Stick', strange as that might sound. He was just a stickboy who wanted to feel like part of the team. He was willing to do something really wrong just so that the other kids would like him. He probably didn't even think about how serious it might turn out. Now he couldn't even brag about it. If he said anything to anybody, his goose was cooked! He would be in trouble, bigtime!

I told Ned what I was thinking--that I felt kind of sorry for 'Stick. Ned just shook his head. "I don't believe it!" he exclaimed. "You feel sorry for him? Well, that's fine. Feel sorry for him all you want. Just don't trust him, that's all."

"Okay."

"It's going to take more than 'Okay,'" Ned said. "Promise me you won't trust him. You don't have to be mean to him, but promise me you won't trust him."

"Okay, okay," I told Ned. "If it makes you feel better, I won't trust him."

"It makes me feel better," Ned said, laughing. "I didn't know you cared how I felt," he said, kidding me.

For the next couple of days, 'Stick' kept acting as friendly as could be. I tried to act as normal as I could. What Ned had warned me about might be true. But then, maybe Ned might be wrong, and I might be right. There was no way to really know. All I know is that we are supposed to forgive people. So even though I kept Ned's warning in mind, I tried to act friendly to 'Stick.'

As it turned out, 'Stick' was going to need a friend. He was about to get himself into trouble. Ned didn't even need a plan this time.

It happened when we were in Mr. Cameron's class. We were still on that topic about teams and cities. Different groups had huge rolls of paper, and we were supposed to make a mural about teams and cities. As usual, 'Stick' comes over to where I am, and he decides to work right next to me. He didn't say anything at first, but other kids were talking, so it didn't seem unusual. On stuff like this, Mr. Cameron allowed kids to talk out loud, as long as they kept their voices low. We were kneeling on the floor, so we could reach different parts of the mural. Mr. Cameron was kind of moving from section to section, stopping to look at what different groups of kids were doing. I was kind of minding my own business, when 'Stick' suddenly starts talking to me, acting really friendly. What he started saying made me think of Ned's warning. "I sure am glad that you got out of trouble," 'Stick' says.

I was kneeling on the floor, wondering what on earth made him say that.
We hadn't even been talking to each other. For him to suddenly talk about the trouble didn't make any sense. Then I noticed this large pair of shoes, right next to us, and I knew that Mr. Cameron was standing there, looking down at our work.

But that wasn't all. He kept talking, even louder. "Y'know, Nate, I knew you weren't the one who wrote that note to Demski. If you were the person who sprayed MacIntyre's car, you wouldn't be dumb enough to write about it in a note!"

I couldn't believe it! He didn't even realize what he was saying! Nobody knew what was in that note, except the people who were in that office. They were the only ones who knew that the note had stuff in it about the spray paint on the car!  The only other person who could have known that had to be the person who wrote the note!

I'm sure my head must have snapped around so fast that you'd think I would have broken my neck.  Had Mr. Cameron heard what 'Stick' had just said?  And if he heard it, would he know that only the guilty person would know what 'Stick' knew?

The look on Mr. Cameron's face answered my question!  It was a look of total amazement.  Mr. Cameron kind of blinked, opened his eyes really wide, and stared at me as if to say, "Did you hear that!"  This time, I didn't need Ned to play detective.  'Stick' had just confessed to writing the note, and he didn't even know it!

"Son," Mr. Cameron said to 'Stick,' taking him by the elbow and lifting him to his feet. "Come with me, please."

'Stick' is looking totally bewildered--like somebody who knows something is terribly wrong, but who doesn't have any idea just exactly what it is.  You could tell that he couldn't even think, because he walked out of the room with Mr. Cameron like he was a robot or something.

About two seconds later, Ned is by my side.  That guy never misses anything!   He picks up a brush and pretends to be working on the mural. "What's going on!" he murmurs. Everybody else was so busy drawing and talking that they missed the whole thing. But not Ned.

"What was that all about?" he mumbled. "What's going on?"

"Stick just confessed," I whispered.

"What!" Ned exclaimed. "Confessed! I don't get it!"

This time I felt like the detective.

"I'll tell you after class," I said. "This'll really get you!"

The last kid was hardly out of the room when Ned demanded to know every detail.

"There's really not much to tell," I said, trying to act like I found it to be quite simple. "You're the one who warned me that 'Stick' was only acting friendly." Ned nodded.

"'Stick' was trying to put on a show for Mr. Cameron. Right when Mr. Cameron gets next to us, 'Stick' confesses."

"You gotta' be kidding," Ned said. "Why would he confess?"

"He didn't actually confess," I told Ned. "At least, he didn't know he confessed." I told Ned what 'Stick' had said, including the part about what was in the note.

"Ned," I told him, "Nobody knew what was in that note. The only people who knew what the note said were Mr. Cameron, Mr. Stelvin, my Dad, the police officers, and the two of us! Even the secretary didn't have time to read it. Ned, nobody else knew. Except the person who wrote the note. What 'Stick' said to me was just as good as a confession. He couldn't have known what was in the note unless he wrote it himself!"

Before Ned could ask even one more thing, Mr. Cameron came back into the room.

"Ned," Mr. Cameron said, very seriously, "I need to ask you a direct question. First I will tell you that 'Stick' is in the principal's office. We think he wrote the note. There is no way he could have known what was in it unless you or Nathan told him."

Ned was shaking his head, as if to say, "I didn't tell him!"

Mr. Cameron ignored him. "We know that you and Nathan would not have said anything about what was in the note. So we are quite sure that 'Stick' wrote it. He is quite scared right now. But I don't want to make the same mistake twice," Mr. Cameron said, looking at me. "I don't want to jump to conclusions, like I did when Nathan was caught with the note.

Ned was frowning, wondering what was coming next.

"One thing would give me a lot more peace of mind about this," Mr. Cameron continued. "Ned, I know that you know who is behind this. I would like you to consider telling me whether 'Stick' is the boy you overheard in the washroom. I won't tell anyone that you told me. I don't want to put you into any danger with any other kids. I just need to know for my own sake."

Ned looked at me, as if to ask me what he should do. But this was his decision. He would have to make up his own mind.

"Ned?" Mr. Cameron repeated.

"'Stick'," Ned said, softly.

"You're sure?"

"Yes, Sir. I'm sure."

At last! The whole thing was cleared up. Finally! I could give my complete attention to the championship game.

## Chapter Fourteen: One Man to Beat

When the truth came out about 'Stick,' I could hardly believe how much better I felt. Even though they said they knew I was not guilty, it was good to know that they had proof. It turned out that 'Stick' told them everything. One thing was sure. Stick wouldn't be at the big game. Not even as a stickboy.

The day of the game finally came! We were supposed to be at the Amphitheater two hours ahead of time. That was unusual, because an hour was plenty of time to get equipment on, get last minute instructions, and do warmups. In a way, I was glad we had to be there early. The night before, I didn't even want to eat. The only reason I ate anything at all is because Mom insisted. "You'll need your energy tomorrow morning," she said, "and the time to start getting it is tonight." So I forced myself to eat. Some of the guys said that it was good to eat a lot of spaghetti the night before, so that's what I asked for.

You can probably imagine that I didn't sleep a lot, either. I kept having these dreams, where I couldn't see the puck. In my dreams, it seemed like the lights in the arena were really dim. I kept looking for the puck, but I couldn't find it. When I would find it, I would try to skate, but my skates were dull, and I kept falling down. It was so bad that I even dreamed that I was praying. You can't believe how relieved I was when I woke up!

By the time Mom got ready to call me, I was already dressed and ready to go. She made me drink some orange juice for breakfast, but that was it. Dad threw my stuff into the car and we headed out. Mom would come later.

"You can do it!" she yelled, as we pulled out of the driveway. One thing about Mom. You never ever heard her say anything except encouraging stuff.

I thought for sure that I would be the first guy there, but I could see cars in the parking lot, and some of the other kids' parents were already in the lobby. Dad swatted me on the rear end and said, looking serious, "Go get'm!" He knew how important this game was to me. I hadn't told him anything about Development Camp, because I was almost afraid to think about it. It was hard enough not to talk about the game all the time at home. If I would have told them about Development Camp, I would have had to answer more questions than I was ready to. Besides, I didn't want Mom and Dad to get their hopes up for me. I thought there was a chance for Development Camp, but not a real good one. Still, I could always hope.

I had never seen the dressing room quite like it was. Nobody was saying anything. This was deadly serious business. Something besides the silence bothered me, too. Demski's locker was empty. To me, that wasn't a good sign. I figured that if Coach Arnold thought Demski would make it on time after detention, Demski's gear would be laid out and ready for him. To me, Demski's empty locker meant that Billy Benton would have to play the whole game. He was already suiting up, and he looked nervous. Coach Arnold had let his Dad come into the dressing room to calm him down. Even with his dad, Billy looked like he was shook up. I tried not to think about not having Demski, but my hands were shaking as I took my stuff out of my duffel bag. "Gotta' be cool, gotta' be cool," I kept saying to myself. "Gotta' be cool. The guys might be watching you. Act cool, even if you're not."

Coach Arnold was one smart dude. He knew how shaky we'd be, so he had us come to the arena 'way early so we could have two warmups. Of course, we didn't know that, but that's why he told us to come so early.

"Okay, boys," he said, when we were all dressed. "We're going to go out on the ice for a few easy laps. No pucks. No warmups. I just want you to get out there and skate around. Pretend that you're skating around a lake someplace. Nice 'n easy. No sprints, no nothing. Just skate around the rink four or five times, and head back in."

Coach knew what he was doing. We made our way down the ramp and onto the ice. They didn't even have all of the rink lights on yet. A handful of people were in the seats, but the arena was empty. Still nobody said a word. You could hear the skates kinda' squeaking on the ice, and since there was nobody in the arena, the sound made a strange echo. Each guy was thinking serious thoughts. After about five easy times around, we headed for the ramp again. I was surprised to discover that I was breathing hard, in short, quick breaths. But so were the other guys. "Nerves--" Dad would say later. "When people get nervous, they have trouble catching their breath. Coach Arnold was squeezing all of those nerves out of you guys 'way before you were even going to go out for warmups."

Back in the dressing room, it seemed like everybody was lined up to go to the bathroom at the same time. "Weird," I thought. "I don't remember anything like this ever happening before a game. But I had to go, too."

By now there was a little bit of noise in the dressing room. Guys started to talk in low sounds. Then, after a few minutes, they were talking in normal voices. Even Billy Benton was talking, and his Dad wasn't in the dressing room anymore.

I felt a lot more calm now. Relaxed, almost. I took the time to tighten my skates and say another little prayer. The dreams about not being able to see the puck, and skates that were too dull, seemed far away.

I must have been concentrating really hard. I didn't see anyone come into the dressing room, but when I looked up from tying my skates, I could see Coach Arnold and a stranger standing just outside the door. I had seen that man some place before. Then it hit me! He was one of the two men I saw at practice at the old Olympic Rink. He was one of the men I thought were scouts!

Everybody knew that Coach Arnold was a good friend of the scout for Development Camp. They had played together years before in the International Hockey League, and they had kept up their friendship throughout the years. So it was no big surprise that the scout had come to wish Coach Arnold luck. What was puzzling was that they seemed to be having a very serious conversation. I couldn't help but see that, and it wasn't that I was staring at them or anything. I wasn't. In fact, I made a special point of it not to look at them. I tried to keep my head down, and I messed with my skate laces. But I could see out of the corner of my eye. From the way coach and his friend were standing, and from how Coach Arnold turned, a couple of times, to look into the dressing room, I got a funny feeling. Could they be talking about me?

You know how you feel when you think somebody is talking about you? Well, this was worse, because I couldn't figure out what they could possibly be talking about. For sure it couldn't be Development Camp. Everybody was saying that the scouts had already picked two players from every league. I had heard that they had only one spot left for somebody from our league. And, of course, everybody knew that Biggy Benzin was at the top of their list. So I couldn't figure out what they might be saying about me.

I was soon to find out.

The stranger patted Coach on the back and headed out to the arena. "Okay!" Coach Arnold hollered at us, "Hear this!"

Coach gave us his usual "burn-up-the-ice" talk. But there was something different going on this time. I couldn't quite tell what it was, but even Coach Arnold seemed to be nervous. For one thing, he seemed to be holding his breath when he was talking. Like he wasn't breathing normally. For another thing, he was walking back and forth. He never did that before a game. He always stood by the doorway so he could smack each guy on the rear end as we headed out to the ice. And there was something else: He always talked with his hands, and the more excited he got, the more his hands flew around. One time he got so carried away between periods that knocked his own hat off. In fact, for laughs, we used to call him "Puppet Man"--behind his back, of course--because his hands would fly around like somebody was pulling them with strings. But now he had his hands stuffed way down in his pockets, and you could tell that they were curled up into fists.

"Now listen you guys! This is it! There are no second chances! Nobody expects us to win! We're not gonna' prove that we deserve to be in the championship game. We're gonna' prove we're the champions! We're gonna' go out there, we're gonna' skate with 'em, we're gonna' hit with 'em, we're gonna' dig for every puck, fight for every inch of ice, steal every face-off, beat 'em to every corner, and take charge of this game until the last whistle blows. If we get knocked down, we're gonna' get up. If we get ahead, we're gonna' stay ahead. If we get behind, we're gonna' fight back. If we can't match 'em man-for-man, we'll match 'em check for check, hit for hit, guts for guts. We're gonna' show 'em what happens when a real *team* plays together. We're going to skate until our lungs burn, and if you're not puking by the time we have a line change, your not puttin' out! Now get out there and show 'em how to play hockey!"

If he would've been at his usual spot at the ramp entrance, Coach Arnold would have been knocked over! The guys practically leaped off the bench and poured forward like a tidal wave. The hollering in the dressing room was like nothing I had ever heard before! I wasn't the only one who actually believed we they could win! Coach was right. Like the Bible says, a single strand is quickly broken, but when strands of rope are bound together, nobody can break it! We were a team! Nobody could break us!

I think I would have rocketed out of there at the head of the pack, but coach grabbed me so hard by the arm he practically yanked me backward. "Nate," he said, looking down at me really hard. "Development Camp is interested in you. The man at the door was my old teammate, Scout MacDonald. He wasn't in here only to wish me good luck. He told me that they have one spot open for a player from our league. They've had their eye on Biggy Benzin. But they heard about that winning goal you scored last game. It caught their attention.

They're watching you, too, now, Nate. They like your speed and determination. It's down to this: It's Biggy Benzin, or you."

Coach looked at me again. Real hard. Then he said one more thing. And each word came out very slowly.

"You've got one man to beat."

You would have figured that there was no way I could get more hyped up for the game. But man was I wrong! I felt like a human missile. Like somebody filled me full of rocket fuel. At that moment, I could have powered the puck right through the boards!

So here it was. More than the last game of the season! More than the league championship. Development Camp! The chance to be picked by a pro scout! One thing rang in my ears more than the roar of the crowd. Coach's words:

"One man to beat!"

Problem was, I almost beat the wrong man.

## Chapter Fifteen: Now or Never

No faceoff was ever this important. People were screaming before the game even started. Each team had its best players on the ice. One thing I made up my mind to do was to look Biggy Benzin right in the eye when lined up for the faceoff. He would know from the get-go that Nathan Metcalf was not going to back down!

The puck was a flash coming out of the ref's hand. At long last, this was it! I smacked it hard, to my right, and my wingman picked it up. "Dump and chase," Coach Arnold told us. "Dump and chase," he hammered at us, again and again in practice. "We can't beat their defensemen with fancy passes or stickhandling. So we'll dump and chase, and race 'em to the corners. If we play it right, we'll wear 'em out. We're in better condition than anybody. The more we stay even or close to even, the better our chances. The longer we go, the better we get. The longer we go, the weaker they get. The longer we go, the stronger we get. We'll skate 'em into the ice!"

And that's exactly what we did. They'd get the puck, we'd be on 'em in a second. They couldn't move without one of our guys bugging them. One shift on the bench, when I was watching our guys matching them stride for stride, I thought back to Mr. Cameron's class. What was it that Marlene had said--something about liking a gnat because it was a small bug that could drive you crazy. That's exactly what we were. We were swarming around them like a bunch of gnats. We wouldn't leave them alone.They had better players than we had. And they were firing pucks at Billy Benton like he was a target in a shooting gallery. But the thing was, they could never get a clean shot. You could tell they were getting frustrated. Just when they thought they had a shot lined up, one of our guys would get in the way. Or hit their stick. Or steal the puck. You could tell they were getting mad. They started slashing when we'd get the puck, and they started going for the hit when they should have gone for the puck.

By the end of the first period, it was 0-0. In the dressing room, Coach Arnold was back to normal, waving his hands in the air.

"We're tied. Don't even think of being satisfied with that!" he hollered.
"Keeping them out of our goal isn't going to win this game for us. We've gotta' have some offense! If we let 'em keep boxing us in, sooner or later they're going to get lucky. We can't win the game by playing it in our end of the ice! You gotta' keep bugging them, but we've gotta' get some offense. Offense! Now go get 'em!"

I never had an intermission go so fast in my life. I have to admit that I was hoping to stall them, hoping that we could drag things out so Demski could get here. But in the first period, there weren't many whistles. Half the time, we were changing on the fly, and the game was going faster than usual. We were hoping to go real slow when we had line changes and faceoffs, but we didn't even get the chance. The whistles just weren't there! If we could have gotten ahead by at least a goal, we could have iced the puck over and over, and forced faceoffs. But now coach was telling us to get some offense going.

I could tell that Coach Arnold was worried. Between periods, he kept licking his lips, and taking drinks of water from the big cooler in the corner of the dressing room. For some reason, I counted seven paper cups that he threw into the trash. You know how you think of stupid things sometimes, when you shouldn't? Of all things, I thought, "I wonder what he's going to do when all that water goes through him and it's the middle of the second period? Where's he gonna' you-know-what?" Yeah, I know it's stupid, but that's actually what I thought.

Coach Arnold wasn't the only one who was worried. Billy Benton had been great in goal. You couldn't have asked him to play better. He was playing the best he ever had. But we all knew that we were lucky. The Warriors had hit the post twice. Another time, Billy bobbled the puck and it sort of fluttered up and landed on the net, on top of the goal. So we all knew that we could have been behind by three or four goals. As for the rest of us, we didn't even have a decent shot on goal. Billy was good, but we needed Demski. We couldn't keep this up. We not only needed his goaltending. We also needed to hear him screaming like a crazy man.

At the start of the Second Period started, the crowd had simmered down. I think everybody was waiting for the game to bust wide open. Our fans were frustrated, because we would just dump and chase, but we never made anything happen, even when we beat the Warrior players to the puck.. And they knew that we would have to quit playing defensive hockey, or the Warriors would score. Sure enough, that's exactly what happened. I don't think we got the puck out of our end for the first four minutes of the period. Then, all of a sudden, "Bang!"--Benzin let one go from just inside the blueline, and Billy kind of hunched up when the puck hit him. It bounced off him and it was inside the red line. Now we were down. Warriors 1, Blazers 0.

We must have been in shock. The ref drops the puck for the faceoff after the goal, and we win the draw. But the Warriors' right wing, a kid by the name of Wally Snyder, whips in, steals the puck, cuts across the blueline, and lets go a backhand. Billy Benton just plain got beat! In less than thirty seconds, we're down by two goals. You could almost see our guys start to sag.

To make it worse, while we're skating for the faceoff at center ice, I hear this voice beside me. "Eat it, punk!" It was Biggy. And he had the same look on his face that he had before Marlene slam-dunked him in class.

I was really mad! I felt like taking the puck and doing it all myself--jamming it right down Benzin's throat! But Coach Arnold had warned us about forgetting to play as a team. "A team can beat 'em!" he kept telling us. "A good team of hard-working players can beat a collection of all-stars every day of the week, seven days a week." The way he said it, you'd believe him no matter what. But right at this moment, I had other thoughts. All I could think of was, "Get me the puck. Get me the puck! I'll teach that big-mouthed hot dog not to act so cocky."

All this is racing through my head, and my eyes are glued to the puck, waiting. The ref is looking at the timekeeper, the Warriors' fans have stopped screaming, and I'm ready to do it myself. Then I hear Coach Arnold. "Dump and chase, dump and chase!" Coach Arnold is yelling from the bench, before we face off for the third time at center ice. I have to admit, I was starting to wonder about doing dump and chase. We didn't seem to be getting anywhere, but he wanted to stick with that game plan. "Okay," I was thinking. "I'll do it. But if we don't change things, I'll change 'em myself!"

Well, we stuck with Coach Arnold's plan. Maybe it was because the pressure was off, but all of a sudden we were in the Warriors' end about as much as they were in our end. Maybe they got too cocky. Maybe they relaxed. I don't know. But we were actually getting some shots on goal. Then a fluke happens! One of our third line guys is on the ice. He hardly ever gets to play, but Coach Arnold is sticking in a third line guy once in a while to give some of us an extra rest. The third line hadn't played at all. Anyway, this third line kid isn't that great of a skater, but he's a real fighter. He gets the puck and hauls off and whacks it like a golf ball. It hits a Warriors player on the shoulder, goes flying end over end, and bounces into their net! People are screaming and stomping their feet, and coach Arnold is running up and down the bench, pounding our guys on the back, and yelling something I can't even make out.

So now it's 2-1, Warriors, and we're still in the game!

You'd figure that the Warriors would tighten up after that. Well, they didn't. Everybody knew that our goal was a fluke. We even knew it. So maybe they didn't take it seriously. Maybe they were still thinking of their two quick goals. All I know is that they were acting like they thought they could score whenever they wanted to. And it almost seemed like they might. They were really pouring it on, and we were back in our own end again. We were getting hammered. Billy Benton must have thought he was in a blizzard made out of pucks. I knew we couldn't keep this up! I had this sinking feeling that if we went down again, we were gonna' stay down.

The Warriors kept coming at us, and if they were as tired as we were, they didn't show it. The Snyder kid who scored their second goal came flying down the boards with the puck and fired it in. They were doing their own dump and chase! I beat him to the puck and swept around the back of the net, and up toward the blueline, but I was out of gas. I had to get to the bench. Kenny Earl, one of our defensemen, was even with me, so I flipped him a quick pass and headed for the bench, to change on the fly. I was just about there, when I heard this huge roar.

Snyder had scored for the Warriors! Biggy had used a huge sweep check on Kenny, and he hit Snyder with a cross-ice pass. Snyder was wide open, and that was it! We were down 3-1!

I hadn't even made it to the bench! Down 3-1, and we're heading into the end of the Second Period?! Before I could even think about it too much, I hear another roar. I look up, and the linesman is waving his hands, palms down, signaling "No goal!" I looked at Coach Arnold and he was standing up on the bench, screaming, "Off side! Off side!" I guess he thought the officials missed it, but they didn't. Biggy had hit Snyder with a good pass. No question about that. Trouble was, Snyder was offside. So their goal was no goal! Still 2-1! There must have been angels on the ice with us!

I didn't have to get a shift on the bench, because the goal-no goal took enough time for me to get my wind back. I jumped back on the ice for the last couple of minutes of the period, for the faceoff. I'm watching the ref's hand again, when all of a sudden he stands straight up and signals "Time-out." "What is coming off?" I'm thinking. It's Coach Arnold. He called a time out! I couldn't for the life of me figure out what he was doing. Timeouts were for the Third Period. Why call one now? Then I hear another roar, and it's our fans. By now, I'm really confused, because Coach called a timeout, but he's ignoring us. He's looking behind our box. Then I see him! It's Demski! How did he get all his equipment on and get here for the closing minutes of the Second Period?

In the last minutes of the Second Period we played like we had gulped pure oxygen! The guys on the ice were skating like madmen. The guys on the bench were banging their sticks on the boards and hollering like crazy. We were hoping Demski might make it for a few minutes of the Third Period, but this was a miracle. How did Demski get from the school to the arena, from the arena to the dressing room, and how did he get all that gear on so fast?

We were to find out later that Demski wasn't Dumb-ski after all! When it came to thinking his way out of trouble, Demski was as dumb as a fox!

## Chapter Sixteen: Flukes and More Flukes

Almost all sports have their strange moments. A ball takes an unusual hop in baseball, and a team wins a tournament. A freak rebound in basketball, and somebody loses a championship. Football has its fumbles that happen at strange times. And hockey--well, the right bounce at the right time, and everything changes. Of course, that's what happened with our fluke goal.

Between periods, Coach Arnold came right at us. "Okay, I'm not gonna' go easy on you guys. We've had lucky breaks. We got a lucky break on our goal. I'm not gonna' call it a fluke, though, because when you put the puck on net, good things can happen. Good things happened. But now we have to make them happen. We can't let them happen to us."

All eyes were on Coach Arnold. There was new fire in our dressing room. Billy Benton looked relieved. Demski looked like he was about to devour anyone who got in his way. His attitude rubbed off on us. All of a sudden, we were back in the game. Really back. No kidding ourselves. No hoping. Just believing we could really win this one!

"This is where the conditioning pays off," Coach Arnold declared. "They're gonna' be more tired than you are. They expected to be way ahead, and they're not. They'll start to press. They'll make mistakes. Dump and chase. You're gonna' start beating them to the puck. Mark my words. The first Two Periods, they kept up with us. Now they'll start to fade. The more they chase, they more they'll fade. We'll stick with our game plan. Sooner or later, we'll chase the puck down and we'll have a man open in the middle, and we'll put it away. Play for a tie this period. Play for a tie. Don't worry about trying to win. We need one goal. Play for an Overtime. If we get 'em into overtime, we'll knock 'em out. They won't have any legs left, and they won't have any wind left. You're in better condition. Okay, let's go! Let's have your hands!"

The guys poured into the middle of the dressing room and grabbed hands. "Think 'One Goal!'" Coach yelled.

Demski was just what we needed. Third Period started off in a mad rush, and stayed that way. It was a seesaw battle. First we'd get into their end, then they'd break out and attack our end. We'd recover and clear the puck, and dump it into their end. Coach was right. We started to beat the Warriors to the puck, and we started getting more shots on goal. Demski was sensational. You could almost feel that nothing was going to get past him. He was fresh, and strong, and full of fire. He acted like he could've caught a bullet, he was so quick and so determined.

The minutes were ticking off the clock. Time seemed to be standing still and racing by at the same time. I know that sounds stupid, but that's how I felt. But the racing by feeling was stronger.

I don't know why, but in this game, I seemed to miss the biggest moments. Just like when I missed the goal-no-goal that Snyder had scored for the Warriors. I was on the bench, and grabbing for a water bottle. All of a sudden, our fans start yelling, and when I looked up, I couldn't believe it!

Kenny Earl, our other really good defenseman, had done a "give-and-go" with our left winger on our second line. They had a two on one, and he had a breakaway. Biggy wasn't on the ice then, either, for the Warriors, and Kenny came tearing in on their second string defense. The kid who was playing left defense might have gotten beat by Kenny--I don't know, because Kenny wasn't that fast--but whether he did or not, it didn't matter. When Kenny started around him, the kid shot his arm out to make a check, and he lost his grip on his stick. It slid right across Kenny's line of fire. Coach said later that it looked like an honest mistake--like the kid just accidentally lost control. From where the ref was, though, it looked like he threw his stick to stop Kenny. But here's where some major luck came in. Kenny has a point-blank shot, and he misses! The shot goes wide--doesn't even hit the goalie. But the lucky part is, just as he's whipping it off, the whistle goes. He gets a penalty shot because of the flying stick!

You'd figure that with that kind of pressure, a kid would blow it. Not Kenny! Kenny Earl never misses twice in a row. Everybody's screaming like crazy and you can't tell who's screaming what, because their fans are trying to make him nervous, and our fans are trying to encourage him. He must have been deaf, because he was so cool you wouldn't believe it. He races in and fakes a shot. The goalie goes down, in a butterfly, and Kenny smashes it in at the top of the net! In that split second, everything changed. It was a brand-new hockey game. We had new life!

## Chapter Seventeen: Sudden Death

So now we're back in the game. Now the clock wasn't our enemy any more. The Warriors started making mistakes. They were frustrated and desperate. Who could blame them? Here they were, pouring on the pressure, and we come back and get even on two crazy goals. Anybody would get discouraged.

I knew that Coach Arnold was playing for Overtime. That sounds crazy, but he really, truly believed that we were in better shape. If we went to overtime, he thought we'd have something left, and the Warriors wouldn't.

So every time we're changing shifts, he says, "Stay cool. Clear the zone and put the puck in their end. Make 'em work to get it back out." That's exactly what we did. Our team was like a machine, with every part fitting together perfectly.

I don't know when it exactly happened, but at some point you could tell that the Warriors had changed their game plan. With Demski in goal, they stopped peppering the net with shots, and they started passing more, looking for good shots. Trouble was, they were trying for the perfect pass and the perfect shot, and any time you do that, you lower your chances of scoring. Not only that, you set yourself up for a steal. The guys checking you are playing the pass, not the shot, so they're looking for a steal and a breakaway.

Time was running out. If somebody scored at this point, it was all over. As close as this game was, it would take major luck to come back. With all the breaks we already had, I didn't think we could count on more luck. I was just hoping we could hang on. The way the Warriors were pressing, I was starting to wonder.

As we were jumping on the ice, I knew that this would be the last shift of the game. One minute, eight seconds on the clock! Coach Arnold would keep the first line on the ice, no matter how fast the pace. He couldn't afford to go with anything but our best players. The faceoff was at the circle off the right side of our net. Demski was shouting orders like a general in a war.

The Warriors' defensemen were pinching in further than usual. It looked like a power play, except that we weren't short-handed.

The draw went to the Warriors, and Biggy's partner snapped it up. Over to the corner. Then to the back of the net. Then to the corner. They were almost toying with us. Then to the blueline. Except that this time, they got too fancy for their own good. Our wingman intercepts the pass and breaks out. Coach Arnold is bellowing, "Dump and chase! Dump and chase!" I cut up the ice as fast as I could, and, sure enough, the pass is right on the money! This was a repeat of the last game of the season! Almost a laser copy of the play that beat the Warriors. Even to the part with Biggy Benzin racing back to his own end. I found out later that everybody in the arena was on their feet, including the players in both boxes.

Now I've got full control of the puck, and Benzin is racing ahead of me, spinning around to face me on his blueline. I could hardly believe it! I knew I could do it again--"bait and switch"--and put this game away! "I deked you before, and I can deke you again!" I thought. Then I hear it one more time. "Dump it! Dump it!"

I don't know how so many things can race through your mind so fast, but they can. When I heard Coach Arnold yelling "Dump it!" a whole avalanche of stuff went flying through my head: "He's crazy. I can beat this guy! I can put the game away! I can show the scouts what I have! I'll go to Development Camp. I can score! There's just one man to beat!"

You'll never believe this. Just as I'm about to make my big move on Biggy, I think of Dad. His big deal was that you obey your elders. Period. You obey people who have authority over you. What would Dad say?

That's all it took. I was just far enough from Biggy to slap the puck past him into the corner, and watch our wingman chase it in. And that's all I remember.

# Chapter Eighteen: Strange Happenings

The stinging feeling in my cheekbone was what woke me up. I could hear some voices, and then I noticed a bright light overhead. I still had my equipment on, except for my skates. I was on my back. I could hear voices, but it took a couple of seconds before they made any sense to me.

"This has got to be the craziest hockey game I've ever experienced." It was Coach Arnold. I turned my head and tried to focus my eyes. There were two men standing with him at the side of the room. A guy in green was grinning at me. He helped me into a sitting position. My legs were dangling over the side of this table. I noticed that I had my shoes on, but I couldn't remember how I got skates off, and shoes on. In fact, I didn't even know what I was doing here.

"You're going to have a shiner there for a couple of days, son," he said. I put nine stitches right at the side of your nose. And if I were you, I wouldn't be blowing my nose right away. Even after you take out the cotton, it will feel like it's stuffed. That other kid's stick caught you right under the eye and across the shnoz. One thing is sure. You're not gonna' win any beauty contests for a few days. You're swelled up pretty good."

Dad and Coach Arnold were grinning, too. And the other man was nodding, with a big smile on his face. It was Scout McDonald!

They must have all noticed the confused look on my face. Before I could even ask, I was getting the full story.

"Nate," Coach Arnold said, "I wish you could have seen the end of the game."

All four men laughed. Whatever it was, it must have been funny, but I still didn't know what was coming off.

"When Coach Arnold yelled 'Dump it! Dump it!' you looked like you were going to ignore him and put a move on Biggy Benzin."

"Biggy was waiting for you," Coach Arnold added. "What you and I didn't know--or I would have told you--was that when Scout MacDonald was at practice at the old Olympic Rink, the Warriors' coach was with him."

"So the two men at the Olympic weren't scouts!" I thought. "Only one of them was! The other one was the Warriors' coach! And when I showed them everything I had, the Warriors' coach knew what I could do!"

Dad interrupted my thoughts. "They had practiced stopping your 'bait and switch' move. The Warriors' Coach showed Biggy how to hold his stick back a little further than usual on his hip. What you didn't know was that they were expecting you to try it again. When you would have put the puck out there, at the usual distance, Biggy would have nailed you. He would have stolen the puck and had a breakaway."

The Scout was nodding. He hadn't said anything so far, but now he added, "They were waiting--hoping you'd try it again."

"They were so sure," Coach Arnold said, "that you were going to try your move again, they outfoxed themselves. When you dumped the puck in, Biggy wasn't ready for that. He's good enough to recover, and he did. Trouble was, when he swung around to race to the corner, his stick caught you under the visor, and somehow you got cut. Automatic penalty for high sticking. Another 'fluke,' maybe. But a break for us just the same. With their best player off the ice, they got rattled."

"It went just the way Coach Arnold planned," Dad said, looking at Coach with great admiration.

I must have really looked stupid, because the men started to laugh out loud. Scout MacDonald poked Coach Arnold. "We forgot!" he laughed.
"Nate doesn't know how the game ended. He wasn't there!"

Dad gave me the rest of the details. The high-stick had knocked me off my feet, and knocked me groggy enough that they figured I didn't know where I was. I wasn't knocked out, but I was enough out of it that I didn't know what was going on. They took me to the nearest emergency room, which was where we were, now. When the Overtime started, the Warriors seemed to fall apart. Biggy had a double minor, and the guys were able to put on the pressure. All of Coach Arnold's board-puking wind sprints paid off. Our guys had the legs and the lungs, and the Warriors were skating like they were carrying bags of cement. With eight seconds left in Biggy's penalty, there was a mad scramble in front of the Warriors' net, and somebody banged it in. It might have even been a Warriors' player. Kenny Earl got the credit, but nobody really cared. The "Dump and Chase" strategy had paid off.

But what was Scout MacDonald doing at the hospital? I could understand why Coach Arnold was here with Dad, but why Scout MacDonald.

He must have read my mind. "Son, he said, I came to the hospital to personally invite you to Development Camp."

Was I hearing him right? I never had a chance to show him what I could do with the puck against Biggy Benzin.

"One of the things we're looking for in our prospects is talent, of course. But we are also looking for players who are able to listen to instructions. Players who are willing to listen, to do what they're told, and to learn." He stuck out his hand, and shook mine.

"You might have been able to beat Biggy Benzin on that last rush. Personally, I think they were ready for you. You had one man to beat. You could have tried to beat the man on the blueline--Biggy Benzin. But you made a good choice. You followed your coach's instructions. Son," he said, "you beat the right man. The man you had to beat was yourself. You put your coach first, and yourself last. You put your team ahead of yourself. That's what we're looking for. Team players with talent."

I think I was in shock again! I didn't know what to say. Before I could think of an answer, Scout MacDonald was shaking hands with Dad and Coach Arnold. As he was leaving, he turned and said, "I'll be looking for you at camp! Here's hoping you don't look quite as ugly by then," he joked, with a big wink.

What a strange morning! Nine stitches and a black eye! Development Camp! The championship game! Overtime that I didn't even get to see! Life was full of surprises!

But there was one more surprise that had nothing to do with hockey, and it would make me forget all about my stitches and my shiner.

## Chapter Nineteen: Thinking Fast

Of course, getting hurt is no fun. But I can't say it's all bad. In fact, there's one part of it that is kinda' good. Because if you're gonna' get hurt, there's always all the attention you get from your Mom. And boy, did she give me the attention! When Dad went to emergency with me, Mom had to get home to take care of the rest of the kids. By the time Dad and I got back, the family room looked like a New Year's party. Naturally, Mom had to fuss over me and make me sit down and, of course, eat. I don't know how she knew it, but there in front of me was the one thing I would have wanted more than anything: a huge vanilla milkshake, with at least two refills waiting. I have to admit that I acted like I was suffering a little more than I really was. But moms seem to like fussing over their kids.

So I kinda' felt like I was doing her a favor. Well, not really. But I figured that if she thought I was doing a little bit of acting, she wouldn't mind.

Sleeping that night was tough. Every time I would roll over onto the side with the stitches, I would wake myself up. My cheek was throbbing. But then, I'd start thinking about all the good stuff, like the championship, Development Camp, and everything else, and I'd be asleep again.

Whether I had stitches and a black eye or not, when morning came, Dad made sure we were all out of bed in time to go to church. I was sorta' hoping he'd feel sorry for me and let me stay home. I should have known better. It didn't matter where we lived, we went to church the first Sunday we were there. The only time you got to miss was if you had something like a cold or the flu, or something other people would catch from you. Stitches and a black eye weren't contagious. So I had to go to church. Don't get me wrong. I was thankful to the Lord that we won the game and all, but I could have been just as thankful staying home. As it turned out, I was glad I went. And it wasn't the sermon or the music.

I confess. I don't have a clue what the sermon was about. What was in my head was hockey. I know that wasn't the sermon! I tried, but I just couldn't concentrate. I don't even know how long the service lasted. It seemed like we came in, we sat down, we sang, we listened, and it was time to leave. That fast.

There were enough people who came up to us after church to ask what happened to me, that we were about the last ones out. When we got to the door, Pastor Tim says, "Mr. Metcalf, can you and your son stay for a couple of minutes? I'd like to ask a favor of you."

Dad looks at me, kinda' curious. Then he shrugs his shoulders and says, "Sure. My wife wants to visit with some of the women anyway."

Pastor Tim says good-bye to the last person, and then turns toward his office. Dad and I followed him, and when we get there, I see that it's not the usual kind of office you'd expect in a church. There's a pop machine in there, and a bunch of sports pictures. Pastor's into skiing and outdoors stuff, and he usually leads a summer retreat for kids. He flips me a quarter and says,

"Have a pop. I still have to use quarters, but I have the key, so I get 'em all back."

While I'm trying to decide what kind of pop I want, Pastor Tim says to Mom and Dad, "Mr. and Mrs. Metcalf, this is kind of an unusual request. First, I want to tell you that I know all about the incident at school-- the spray paint thing."

I spun around like somebody had me on a rope. How could he know that?

Pastor Tim's smile set me at ease. "No, it's not anything bad. I had to hear about it. You see, several months ago, my wife and I were approached by Social Services. They told us that they had a young man who had been in a number of foster homes. He was having a hard time getting along with any of his foster parents. He had no friends. Social Services knew that I like kids. My wife is a friend of the head of the department, and the lady there knows that we have no kids of our own. Well, one thing led to another, and they asked us to take this kid in. We did. He was doing fine. We even got him involved with some sports. He had never played, but he liked to be a part of a team. We were able to get him in as a helper on one of the hockey teams. He still wasn't able to make too many friends. But the kids on the team at least talked to him. They even gave him a nickname. He liked it. They called him 'Stick.'

I felt like the whole Warriors team high-sticked me! 'Stick!'

"He was the stickboy for the Warriors. Well, Mr. Metcalf, you know the rest of the story. He got into serious trouble. The judge and the probation officer recommended that he be released to the care of my wife and me. On one condition. That we try to get him paired with some kids who might be a good influence on him."

Dad and Mom looked at each other.

"This is where you come in, Nate. We know that 'Stick' wanted to get you into trouble. So, in a way, you could say that he's your enemy. But I'd like to ask that you and your parents consider our request. I'd like to know whether you can forgive 'Stick'--even if he doesn't ask for forgiveness--and room with him at church camp."

"We really don't need to think about it at all, Pastor," Dad was saying. Mom was nodding in agreement. "It's up to Nathan. We will understand if he doesn't want to do it, and we'll support him if he does do it."

I wasn't sure about this at all. But I didn't know what to say. I took a long swallow of pop and stared at the floor. How can I be this kid's friend?

What if he still acts like a jerk? I was about to say that I needed time to think about it.

"I realize that this is a big favor, Nathan," Pastor Tim was saying. "There are two people who can tell you a little bit about 'Stick.' One of them is our youth pastor, and the other person is the president of our youth league. They'll both be at the camp. And they'll both be working with you every day."

"Well," I said, looking at Mom to rescue me, but Mom just sat there, waiting for me to make my decision. "Well . . . ."

"Let's make it a bit easier," Pastor Tim said, jumping out of his chair. The youth pastor and the president are down the hall. Why don't I just call them in here and you can meet them. Then, you can take your time making a decision. You can ask them what you want, and you can take all week to make up your mind. Take all the time you want, in fact."

I couldn't very well say 'no' to that. So Pastor Tim goes down the hall, and I sit there looking at Mom and Dad. I know that they're hoping I'll do it.

One thing about them, though, is that they would never force me to do something like this.

"Nathan," Pastor Tim says, "Meet Pastor Mike, the youth pastor."

"Hi," I said, sticking out my hand.

"Hi," he says. "The president of the youth group will be here in a second."

I can't remember what he started talking about. I also can't remember anything else. In the middle of a sentence, he stops and turns.

"There she is," he says.

I turned toward the door.

And there were *those eyes*.

"Nathan," Pastor Mike says, "I'd like you to meet Marlene."

Suddenly I knew I wouldn't need too much time to think about summer retreat.

After all, a guy has to think of others, doesn't he?!

## The End

If you liked this book, and want to see more
books like it, ask your school or your
library or your bookstore to order it.

The order number is
ISBN 0-9673697-2-X